May 21st

ALWAYS VICTORIOUS

By Tim Mario Christian

TO CONSTANTINE THE GREAT

"But the Slavs, who started their incursions into the Balkan Peninsula in the 6th century [AD], had by the end of the 7th century [AD] transformed the ethnic structure of all the Illyrian-speaking territories. Croatia, Serbia, Dalmatia, Bosnia, Montenegro, and parts of Macedonia lost their Illyrian language and were thoroughly Slavonized, so that only the Albanians remain as direct descendants of the ancient Illyrians."
(Encyclopedia Britannica Online)

CHAPTER 1

THE ILLYRIAN COURAGE

AS THE SUN arose in the east of Nikomedia, Constantine did not wake up as usual. The hard training with other soldiers of Diocletian's army the day before had exhausted him. While he was sleeping in his own house, a morning dream came to him. In it, he was a little boy again, riding in a forest, surrounded by high trees, returning home with some killed birds in one hand and a bow and arrow in the other. Suddenly, three Roman soldiers led by their commander appeared around him with the tips of their swords pointed at him menacingly.

They talked to him in a deep harsh voice.

"You have been illegally hunting in the property of Emperor Diocletian."

'Soldiers, I am the son of Emperor Constantius, adopted by Emperor Diocletian just a few days ago. I have the right to hunt here," tear-eyed ten-year-old Constantine told them.

"Oh yes? You, the son of the Emperor? Very funny! You know that lashes await little liars," the commander said and laughed loudly.

Flashes of a man who had been whipped in the square the other day, his skin breaking and blood starting to gush out, passed through young Constantine's mind. He knew he had to defend himself.

"I am not a liar. I have done nothing wrong. Why would you beat me up?" asked Constantine

"Well, just for fun, then" the commander mocked him and laughed again. The soldiers joined in the laughter too.

Constantine looked at them in surprise, not understanding what was going on.

"You are not the son of Emperor and you cannot hunt here," said one of the soldiers.

"You are making a big mistake. My mother Helen told me I could hunt here. She does not lie to me," said Constantine.

"You look more like the son of a slave. And we caught you ruining our Master's wealth," said the same soldier.

Constantine got angry.

"Once again, let me tell you that I am the son of the Emperor. What business do you have with me? Don't you have cows to look after?" Constantine fearlessly told the soldiers and tried to move his horse forward.

The soldiers stopped him despite the little boy's courage.

"You filthy little liar! Look at you. Look at your dirty torn clothes. Can the son of the Emperor be dressed like this?" said one of the soldiers.

"Hunting is such. You got to get your hands and your clothes dirty," said Constantine.

"We will go with you and talk to your mother. If you are lying, you know you will be whipped," said the soldier.

With Constantine leading them, they soon arrived in front of his house. Noticing the soldiers, mother Helen came out to the gate of the fence that surrounded her two-story house to talk to them.

"What brings you here soldiers?" she asked.

"We caught your son hunting in Diocletian's property," the commander said.

"We just got here recently. Constantine is the son of Constantius and Diocletian has adopted him as his son. He can hunt anywhere he wants," said mother Helen.

The commander snapped at her.

"Watch it! If you are lying, you will get a lot of lashing for yourself," he said.

"You are now bothering me! Don't you have something else to do? Go back to farming soldiers, you don't scare me," said mother Helen.

"If he is not the son of the Emperor, you will pay a high price for your lies," said the commander.

There was not much to do now. He told his friends to turn their horses and leave. They all left in a hurry as Helen and Constantine watched.

Constantine looked at his mother Helen in gratitude.

"Thank you for saving me mother," Constantine said.

"As Bishop Lactantius says, 'the truth sets you free,'" Mother Helen said.

Constantine's morning dream was suddenly interrupted by his wife Minervina shaking his arm gently and saying "Wake up Constantine. It's a beautiful day. The sun's risen long ago."

Constantine raised his head from the pillow and opened his big eyes partially and saw his wife, a dazzling young woman full of joy smiling at him.

"Good morning, sweetheart!" Constantine said and closed his eyes again for a moment.

"Good morning, honey," Minervina said and left him for a few moments. She went to the fireplace to start a fire and make some tea which Constantine liked very much. After a while the tea was ready. She filled a cup and after toasting some bread and fetching some butter and cheese in a plate, she put them on a nearby table.

The tea and the toasted brown bread smelled real good. That was enough to make Constantine open his eyes again and sit up. His wife seemed unusually charming that day, a soul in bliss. That made him feel content. Constantine propped himself on his right elbow. He looked at the fireplace where a big fire was burning and decided to move to a small coach there. He thought again about his dream.

Minervina came and sat opposite him.

"I was in the middle of the dream when you touched my arm. In my dream, I was a little boy. Soldiers wanted to whip me. But my mother saved me. She told me what Bishop Lactantius always tells me, that the truth sets us free."

Minervina smiled happily at him.

"The truth does set us free," she said.

"When will I know the truth then?" asked Constantine.

"Well, God has given us another wonderful day to discover the truth" said Minervina.

"You are sounding a bit like Lactantious now Minervina. But by the immortal god, you are a lovely woman. So it's worth waking up just to be with you. You always make me feel like things are not that bad after all," said Constantine.

"Thank you, honey. So let's start the day with a prayer to God, together, for a moment. Please Constantine!"

"What do you want me to say to God," said Constantine.

"Thank him for the new day," said Minervina.

"You know that in my heart of hearts I want to believe in God, honey, but I am not there yet. I do not have faith in God yet, Minervina. I cannot say that I trust in God."

"You had a dream just before waking up. God can speak in dreams," said Minervina.

"But how do I know for sure," asked Constantine.

"All I can say is that, without faith no one can please God. We must believe that God is real and that He rewards everyone who searches for him. And those who wait on the Lord, will find new strength. They will fly high on wings like eagles. They will run and not grow weary. They will walk and not faint," said Minervina quoting some scripture.

"Fly high on wings like eagles, run and not grow weary, walk and not faint. That is so beautifully put," Constantine said and took a deep breath.

"You should thank him for having made you strong like an eagle," suggested Minervina.

"That's fair. I will say a little prayer," Constantine said and after bowing his head, he started to pray, "God, you are a great God for having given to me the strength of an eagle and having brought Minervina, such a beautiful creature, to my life. My life is definitely better because of her. And thank you for having given us a son, Crispus. Thank you."

Minervina smiled and prayed after him.

"Thank you God for our family. I love my husband Constantine. I love our son Crispus. We are a happy family. Make us love our neighbors as well. Make us love even our enemies. We love you," she said.

After these prayers were said, Constantine started to sip his hot tea.

"Where's our son Crispus?" asked Constantine.

"Outside, making your horse ready for you," Minervina told him.

"He is just six. That could be dangerous for him,"

"Your mother is keeping an eye on him. He loves it. He is such great help already," Minervina said.

"It's nice that the little boy helps too."

Minervina went to another room to fetch Constantine's soldier uniform.

When Constantine finished his breakfast, Minervina returned.

"I am really glad that you are praying to God, Constantine. I really am. Praying means a lot to me. Everyone who asks will receive. Everyone who searches will find. And the door will be opened for everyone who knocks. I know one day God will grant all your desires, even the one to become Emperor," said Minervina

"I am doing it for you sweetheart. I want to become Emperor for you, and for our son. That's why I train hard and fight hard," said Constantine standing up and starting to put on his uniform.

"But you got to be careful. I know you fight like an eagle but you got to watch out. You are raising Diocletian's jealousy some say. And Galerius, his son-in-law's jealousy as well. I heard some noises outside our tent early in the morning and got afraid. I just heard some soldiers say, 'Diocletian wants him dead.'"

"Diocletian wants many people dead. He is always going through a phase," said Constantine.

"I thought they were talking about you," she said, and wrapped her arms around Constantine's shoulders.

"Don't be silly," he said.

Constantine reached his hand and touched her face.

"Don't worry gorgeous," he said.

"I love you! I really love you very much, my lord and master," said Minervina.

"I love you more, princess."

Constantine gave Minervina a kiss. "Don't worry about a thing," he added.

Just at that moment, Mother Helen called from outside.

"Constantine, Constantine! There's a soldier standing in front of the gate of our house and he wants to talk to you," Mother Helen said.

"Tell him to come in," said Constantine.

Shortly, a soldier appeared at the door of the waiting room where Constantine was.

"Diocletian wants all his generals in a council meeting in his palace as soon as possible. There is some news that a Persian army has crossed our borders and is on its way towards Nicomedia."

"I will be there shortly," said Constantine.

The soldier bowed his head in respect and left in a hurry.

"What is going on?" asked Minervina.

"It's not uncommon for Persians to do this. They have been doing this since the times of Alexander the Great, who often saved the west from their attacks. Diocletian is probably gathering us to discuss a strategy for the battle that will soon ensue."

Constantine got ready, doned his armor, and went outside. He looked for his white horse. His mother was doing some work in the small garden of their house. He then noticed his son feeding the horse some green grass in a corner in the back.

"Bring my horse to me," said Constantine to little Crispus.

Crispus did as told. Minervina came out of the house and took Crispus by his hand.

Constantine mounted the horse as Minervina and Crispus watched.

"How do I look?" asked Constantine.

"Like an Illyrian eagle?" said Minervina.

"Take care," said Constantine as he kicked the belly of his horse.

Minervina and Crispus waved at Constantine as he was leaving.

Constantine smiled at them and left.

***

Constantine arrived before the Imperial Palace of Diocletian and was immediately let in. Other young and old generals were there waiting for Diocletian to show up. Diocletian's son-in-law, junior augustus Galerius and senior augustus Maximian were there too. All generals were talking to each-other. They were discussing the Persian army which was getting closer to Nicomedia but did not seem much concerned about it. Constantine actually thought that he was the most concerned one in that group. It seemed to him that the others were underestimating the strength of the Persian army, judging by what they were saying.

As all the generals were talking and laughing around a big table, the Emperor's spokesperson suddenly appeared with a dish of black and white grapefruit in his hand. He put it on the table and started speaking out loud.

"Welcome Emperors Maximian and Galerius! Welcome Generals! Emperor Diocletian will be here shortly. I will give you some updates in the meantime. I will start with breaking news number one," the spokesperson said, putting a grape fruit in his mouth.

"The frontiers of the Roman Empire," he continued, "the so-called Pillars of Heracles in the west and those of Dionyses in the east, the pillars that in antiquity were thought to hold up the sky are now under the power of Illyrians. Illyrians are now in control of the tetrarchy of the Roman Empire, outshining the Greeks and the Latins. Four Illyrian Emperors, two senior Augusti, Diocletian and Maximian, and two junior Augusti, Constantius and Galerius are in charge of it."

"Yeah, dream on," said one of the Generals. "In charge, yes. Outshining anybody, nope."

The spokesperson looked at him and said, "The grandeur of Illyria is unquestionable. A mounted Illyrian is irresistible, able to bore his way through forests and mountains and all strong citadels, even the Chinese wall if they wanted to. They are outshining the Greeks and Latins in bravery at least, if not in literature and arts. The rise of the Illyrian soldiers has been unstoppable. That is for sure."

"I thought you were going to say, able to bore his way through the wall of maidens. That has been unstoppable too," said one of the generals sarcastically.

The spokesperson continued undisturbed. "Barbarians keep attacking us every day. They are a nasty race of people. They smolderingly lust after money and war."

"It seems that they are exactly like us, Illyrians. And they seem to be as strong as us too. We should take them more seriously. The Persian army is almost at the gates of Nicomedia," Constantine said hoping that the generals would focus more on the issue at hand, the imminent war with the Persians.

The spokesperson did not respond again. He smiled at Constantine's remark and continued. "Breaking news number two" and he put another grape in his mouth. "Diocletian has decided to persecute Christians at Byzantium. Pushed by Galerius, he has decreed the worship of only the official gods of the Empire by everybody there. Whoever disobeys will be punished severely."

"I thought all gods are good and we accept all of them. It does not seem like a good move to me," said one of the Generals whose family lived in that area.

"All citizens and all soldiers must worship pagan pelasgic gods there. Diocletian, our god-Emperor, thinks it's his duty to tell people what to do and how to live their lives," the spokesperson said.

"Only pagan gods are good, not the Christian God," said Galerius.

"But all gods should be treated equally by the government. Christians are free people and they can take their free decisions. We have to give people freedom in this regard," said Constantine.

Galerius looked angrily at him for a moment but the spokesperson continued.

"The Emperor has decided this way and he is very serious about this issue. The punishment for disobedience for anyone in Byzantium is grave," said the spokesperson.

Many generals sighed with discontent.

Constantine sighed too and wanted to object to this kind of arbitrarity but the spokesperson did not give him time to say anything.

"Breaking news number three" said the spokesperson as he munched at another grape.

"Why do you eat while you are talking?" asked one of the generals who found this habit a bit distracting and annoying. "You should not do that while briefing us!"

The spokesperson's eyes glowed with cynicism.

"Do you want to tell me how to do my job general? Do I tell you how to do your job, how to fight against the enemy, how to use your sword, your shield, your spear, your bow and what strategy to use in battle? No I don't. That's your call. So let me do my job the way I want to do it. If you want my job, you can apply for it to the Emperor. Right now, I am in charge of this job, and I will do it anyway I like. That's why we are called Illyrians, free men. I am free to do my job the way I want. You are free to do your job the way you want. That's how we find our happiness. Through freedom," the spokesperson said.

The general was not pleased that the spokesperson snapped at him and he showed this in his countenance but he did not reply to his comment.

"So as I was saying breaking news number three, and this is the most important one," continued the spokesperson and he put another grape in his mouth with great satisfaction in his face, "a great Persian army from the east is heading towards Nikomedia, as you all were informed. They are dangerous and they are getting closer by the minute. Diocletian will be here any moment to discuss with you his strategy for the battle. And Generals, if you have any complaints about the way I deliver my news, please speak with the Emperor about this issue," he suddenly diverged. "I think you made your point, smart …. elephant!"- said the General trying to make some fun of the spokesperson's heavy weight. The spokesperson moved his hand like an elephant's trunk to him and left.

At that moment, two soldiers standing in front of the door of the room of Diocletian put their right hands by their heart and straightened their spears they held with their left hands. The bedchamber door opened and Diocletian appeared with his crown on his head and a double-headed eagle scepter in his hand, accompanied by four bodyguards. He went and sat on a high throne.

"I see Galerius is here. Maximian is here too. Is everybody else here?" asked Diocletian

"Yes, Emperor," said the spokesperson. "You can start right away, if you want."

As soon as Diocletian sat down and made himself comfortable, he began to speak in quiet voice. "I am here to reveal our strategy for the battle. The Persians, the barbarians we will be facing soon are unworthy enemies. They are actually unworthy friends too, so much so that I felt that it was even worthless to attack and invade their lands or cooperate with them in any way. But this is how one gets rewarded when one does not attack. We are being attacked and we have to defend. They have been growing stronger in recent years and are daring to even attack our capital in the East, Nikomedia. They outnumber our forces two to one. But our soldiers are better trained and better equipped. I thought they would stop at some point but I was mistaken. They have continued their march and been very successful so far, and getting closer to Nikomedia, the city from where I rule. Can you believe it? So we have to take them seriously now or we will become their pray. We need to face them. The sooner, the better. My strategy for this battle with them is simple. We are going to divide our cavalry in three wings, left, center, and right as usual. We are going to do open battle because we are not afraid of them. Our cavalry will get close to them and engage the enemy from a close distance. We will then turn back and retreat and pretend we are fleeing and as soon as they attack us and lose their discipline, we will turn around and destroy them like cockroaches."

Do you agree with this strategy?

There was a pause for a moment. Constantine started to think about the strategy Diocletian proposed. It would be better to have a more detailed plan, which general was going to be where and take care of what. The plan was too vague and risky. But again he couldn't find the right time to speak his mind because Galerius spoke before him.

"Yes we agree. The Persians are no match for our army. And with your experience and leadership, we are sure to win," he said in a cocksure voice.

The other Generals supported the strategy showing their respect for their Emperor, Diocletian. After all, he had been very successful in the past.

Disappointed, Constantine remained silent. It was pointless to raise any objections at this point.

When the meeting was over, the Emperor and the Generals went out and mounted their horses and rode towards the army that was waiting for them.

When the soldiers saw the Emperor, they started cheering "Diocletian! Diocletian!"

Followed closely by his generals, Diocletian put himself at the head of his army and they all started their march towards their enemy.

***

Riding on camels and horses, the Persian army was approaching from the South-West. The Persian King, the mounted Sassanian ruler, Narses, son of Shapur, surrounded by his bodyguards seemed confident in the strength of his army and their bravery.

"Do you think we can win against Diocletian?" asked one of the King's close cousins riding on his right.

"No doubt cousin. He is no Alexander the Great, even if he is his descendant," said the King in a confident tone. "I know my enemy very well," he added.

King Narsus was a proud man and he did not feel inferior to the Roman Emperor and was as sure of success as him. After a short pause, he started to make fun of Diocletian, trying to prove how well he knew him.

"The Augustus" mother tongue is Illyrian. He is of humble origin. He has only a poor, perhaps, no knowledge of Greek, the second language spoken by citizens of his capital at Nicomedia and the international language throughout the eastern provinces that he regularly tours. He has only an Illyrian peasant upbringing, and decades in the army camps. Latin is his preferred tongue not Greek in his communication with his army, and seeking to make a virtue of his shortcoming, he has made the revival of Latin a core element in his program of cultural renewal. All official business in his court is conducted and recorded in Latin, even in cases when all the parties speak Greek. The new emphasis on Latin is like a hobby for him, even though I wouldn"t call it anti-intellectual. Professors of Latin have been appointed in the imperial capitals. In a nutshell, Diocletian is trying to look civilized when in fact he is just an Illyrian peasant. He is not that smart cousin," Narsus said.

Narsus' cousin laughed at his comment.

The Roman army riding on horses and slowly marching towards them came into view. Both armies were in sight of each other but because the evening was falling, they both decided that was not the best time to start a battle and both decided to postpone fighting for the next day. Both armies retreated to a safe distance.

A night full of anxiety and apprehension kept the guards awake. An attack by any of the armies could occur any time while they were asleep. Guards kept a careful watch of the situation at every minute. But nothing happened.

When the sun rose over the mountains, the armies got combat-ready and got closer to one another. Leaders gave orders to their commanders to arrange their troops speedily. Both of them then moved to the back, leading from behind, where it was safer.

Despite being greater in numbers, the Barbarian army got organized just as fast as the Roman army. The attempt of some Romans to harass the Persians and make them break their line failed. Diocletian had to change his strategy if he did not want to lose the battle. The Persian army marched in line, rattling their shields.

Diocletian and Constantine and the Praetorians retreated to a nearby hill from where they could watch the battle and they began to discuss the situation on the terrain as the battle started and it became more violent, raging mostly in favor of Persians.

Constantine noticed right away that the greatest number of the opposite army were ferociously attacking the right wing of Diocletian's army and told him so.

Diocletian was still hoping that his right wing would tackle the enemy but he was disappointed. Because of their sheer superiority of numbers, the Persians managed to break the Romans" line and were causing much damage. Things were getting a turn for the worse for Diocletian's army. "We need to fix the situation before it's too late," said Diocletian. "We need to send some reinforcements there as soon as possible."

"I think we should attack the Persian King himself. We can surprise him," said Constantine.

"How?" asked Diocletian.

"Give me 50 Illyrian Pretorians," said Constantine.

"50 Illyrians to attack the king? That is a dangerous bravado," said Diocletian.

"We have to act fast," said Constantine.

Diocletian had often seen Constantine perform great feats of dare and do. But the situation this time seemed to him irredeemable and approaching the Persian King, impossible.

"Just fifty Illyrians?" asked Diocletian again, worried that he was going to lose the battle.

"Just fifty, Emperor. Time is running out. We need to take action now, before it's too late."

The Emperor pointed his sword in the direction of the right wing and ordered the Illyrian Praetorians, "Follow Constantine!"

Constantine placed his helmet on his head and turned his horse towards the enemy. He kicked his horse's belly gently and said "hoa" to him. The horse went into a gallop immediately. 50 Praetorians followed closely. The Illyrian soldiers did not need to be briefed. They instinctively knew what had to be done.

With an eagle's eye, Constantine scanned the field looking for the Persian King. He finally spotted him, a man of great stature and strength standing behind his troops. Constantine galloped on the right of the formations, spear in hand. That was the best way to approach the Persian King. A bird was seen flying above them. Both armies stopped fighting for a second to see this group of Praetorians galloping by them fast but keeping a safe distance. Constantine threw his spear it seemed at the bird. It missed it by a bit. But the spear then hit a Persian in his chest as he was trying to aim an arrow in the direction of Constantine. The spear fell him from his camel.

The leader of the Barbarians immediately sent some camel-drivers in their direction and tried to stop them. But they were too slow for the horses. So he decided to send some horses as well. Soldiers of both armies started fighting again angrily with much violence on both sides. Blood started to shed. Neither soldiers, nor animals were spared.

The Praetorians created a wall to protect Constantine as they moved around the Persian army to get closer to the Persian King. The Persian troops were already engaged. So only the King's bodyguards could defend him. But they were no match for the highly trained Praetorians.

Using much force and violence, the Praetorians were able to break the line of the bodyguards and Constantine himself was able to get very close to the King and challenge him. The King was fearless and he rushed towards Constantine. As soon as he approached he raised his axe with both hands and took a swing aiming to cut Constantine's head.

With a quick move, Constantine first ducked the blow of the axe and then caught it with his hand and with the sword in the other he cut the right hand of the Persian King. Both his hand and ax were hurled on the ground.

A terrible outcry came out of the mouth of the Persian King. The armies stopped fighting for a moment and looked at the Persian King. Some of the Romans started laughing. After a short moment, the Persian King fainted and fell to the ground.

Two Illyrian soldiers approached and snatched his body, grabbing him by his arms. The Praetorian squadron then headed back to send their trophy to Diocletian.

After witnessing this, the Roman army regained its courage while the Persians lost theirs. Left leaderless, they soon decided to retreat. This just made things more terrible for them for they soon became easy prey of the Roman army. The battle was over. It was won by the Romans. Many Persians lay dead in the field of the battle covered in their own blood. Roman soldiers started collecting the spoils of war, swords, horses, jewels. Constantine and the 50 Illyrian praetorians returned to Diocletian victorious.

"Way to go Constantine, way to go! We've got a new Alexander here! You never stop amazing me!" an excited Diocletian told Constantine in the presence of all generals and praetorians around him when Constantine returned with the captured Persian King, parading him in front of the Emperor and other generals.

"I just did my duty, Emperor. Here's the Persian King, your slave," said Constantine and pointed at the man.

"You and the fifty Illyrian Praetorians who helped are invited to my Palace tonight," said Diocletian.

"Thank you," said Constantine.

The Illyrian Praetorians cheered when they heard about the party. Constantine joined with them again.

"I heard from the soldiers that you have never rewarded Constantine with anything, Emperor Diocletian," said Maximian, Diocletian's guest.

"No, not really. But I treat him like my real son, even though he is my adopted son. I am grooming him to one day become an Emperor of the east."

"Never rewarded him? I hear he has performed many feats of dare and do for you and Galerius in the past," said Maximian.

"Yes, it's true. Many times. When Constantine was a younger man and was serving in the cavalry against the Sarmatians, he seized by the hair and carried off a fierce savage, and threw him at the feet of Emperor Galerius. Then sent through a swamp by Galerius, he entered it on his horse and made a way for the rest of Romans to the Sarmatians, of whom he slew many and won the victory for Rome," said Diocletian.

"I have heard about this," said Maximian. "We, the four Tetrarchs, each took the title Sarmaticus Maximus IV. And Constantine got nothing. He deserves a medal right away. He is the pride of Illyrian soldiers. He should get "Courage of Illyria"."

"Don't you think this will arise the jealousy of senior Jovian, Emperor Galerius?" asked Diocletian. "You know he is my son-in-law, married to my daughter Valeria," he added.

"It's unlikely. My son Maxentius is married to the daughter of Galerius. All of us tetrarchs are living in complete harmony. That is why we built that porphyry statue, carved from the purple marble, in Egypt," said Maximian.

"I think you are right. And yes, we do look good in that statue, each clasping the eagle-headed hilt of our swords with our left hand. All looking upward, like so many heavenwards-gazing Alexanders, with close-cropped hair, and angular, masculine chins of soldiers. We do get along quite well," said Diocletian.

"Yes, our differences are only minor. Constantius in the west favors Mars or maybe the Christian God, whereas you, me, and Galerius venerate the eastern favorite, Sol Invictus. My son Maxentius, who is still a youth, a little younger than Constantine evidently still hopes that he might one day succeed, and that is why he got married to the daughter of Galerius. Constantine similarly has to become a pawn in the great game. I thought that was the reason why he was dispatched to the east with you Diocletian and Galerius. This is a good time to do something special for Constantine, to encourage him," said Maximian.

Diocletian wondered why Maximian had the idea of Constantine becoming a pawn in the great game of rising to power so soon. What did he have in mind? But he did not want to ask him about it.

"Ok. I will listen to you, Maximian," said Diocletian. "I will reward him. I will give him a medal."

Diocletian did not disappoint Maximian. As soon as they returned to their palace in Nicomedia, during the party he threw for winning the battle against the Persians, where other Maximian and Galerius were present and many praetorians as well, Maximian's young daughter, Fausta, presented Constantine with the medal "Courage of Illyricum."

Maximian himself was the one who presented him with a sword with an eagle-headed hilt. Galerius was jealous about it but he kept a poker face.

#

CHAPTER 2

PERSECUTION OF CHRISTIANS

AFTER THE PARTY was over, Maximian asked Diocletian for a private conversation. Diocletian agreed curious to know what Maximian wanted to tell him.

"Constantine is one of your great young generals. I know that he is already married to Minervina and they both have a son. But in my view, Minervina is not a good match for Constantine. My young daughter Fausta is. She is too young but a few year from now, she will be a perfect match for him. Can you help me complete this match in the future," Maximian said.

Diocletian was surprised that Maximian finally revealed his scheme to him.

"Maximian, you know I have a lot of respect for you, because, when I felt that the Roman Empire was too large to be governed by one man, and I decided to form a tetrarchy, you Maximian were my first choice as co-Emperor. I regarded you then and I still do regard you now, as a faithful friend and military leader. As Emperors we both hold the title of Augustus. You rule the Western part of the Empire. I rule the East. The other two junior Emperors, Constantius and Galerius, rule their designated areas and are under our authority, as Augusti," Diocletian said.

"I do respect you too Diocletian, as you well know. What is your opinion about Constantine? Maybe you don't want this match to happen," Maximian said.

"I see great potential in Constantine. He reminds me of myself when I was young. Like him, I spent much of my young life in military camps and rose in the ranks of the Roman Army until I connected with the co-Emperors of Rome, Carinus and Numerian. I was the commander of the Emperor's personal bodyguard, just like he is at present. I don't know what will happen in the future. Luck and fate are involved too, not just strength and personal skill and will. I rose to power through interesting circumstances. During a war with the Persians, Numerian was killed. I was made Emperor by the troops of the Roman Army after I killed the man who killed Emperor Numerian. His name was Aper, which means boar. This was significant for me because as a young soldier, a prophecy was made that I would be made Emperor after I had killed a boar. Thus, I always felt this lucky coincidence legitimated my rule as Emperor," Diocletian said.

"What about Carinus? What happened to him?" asked Maximian.

"Well, Carinus still stood in my way of becoming Emperor. However, Carinus' own troops turned on the Emperor and killed him. Thus, in 285 AD, I became the sole Emperor of Rome. When I came to power, the Empire had been the product of many years of chaos and instability. I sought to change this. Through political restructuring and reform, I began to re-establish partial balance and peace in the Empire," Diocletian said.

"What exactly did you do?" asked Maximian.

"My first order of business was to restructure the form of political rule. I created the tetrarchy. So, I don't have any problems with Constantine becoming a junior or a senior Emperor in the future. On the contrary, I want him to become Emperor. I consider him as my son, because I do not have a biological son, as you know. I want the best for him," said Diocletian.

"I know you treat him like a son. That is the reason why you got him from Constantius in the first place and you are grooming him to become a junior Emperor and ultimately a Senior

Emperor. These are all great things about him. That is why I am thinking that a match of him with my daughter is good," said Maximian.

"Yes, that is true. But Constantine loves Minervina. A match of Constantine and Fausta at present is impossible, because Constantine himself would be against it. But in the future, who knows what can happen? I wouldn't rule it out," said Diocletian.

"Thank you Senior Augustus Diocletian. That is all I wanted to hear tonight. Thanks again for your advice," Maximian said.

"Good night Maximian," Diocletian said.

Diocletian was not much surprised that Maximian wanted to make a match between Constantine and Fausta. Constantine was showing signs of greatness at such a young age and everyone thought that there had never been such a great one in a long time. All respected him. His popularity soared every day.

"The match can happen," Diocletian said to himself as he went to bed that night.

In the morning, Diocletian decided to meet with the captured Persian King.

The Persian King had been brought to Diocletian's Palace and was being kept in a room surrounded by guards. The doctors had tied his cut hand with bands.

When Diocletian entered his room, the Persian King fell to his knees.

Diocletian told him to stand up and sit on a chair nearby. He then asked the Persian King what he thought about the battle.

"You army is better Emperor Diocletian. You won fair and square," the Persion King said.

Then Diocletian asked him about Constantine, his adopted son.

"In your view, is he a great warrior?"

The Persian King acknowledged it immediately before Diocletian.

"I have never seen anybody like Constantine before. He is like a lion, sure of his strength, that does not care about the rain of arrows and javelins thrown at him. He attacks, eyes blazing, killing all on his way," the King said.

Diocletian was flattered. He was glad the King said nice words about him and his son Constantine.

Diocletian told the King about his terms of peace.

The Persian King Narsus accepted the terms and decided to become a subject of the Roman Emperor. As a result, Diocletian was soft with him. He even let the King instruct him on how to create a magnificent court.

King Narsus" advice, to make radical changes in his imperial court made Diocletian reflect. He did not make a decision right away but he thought about the King's words: "Diocletian, permit yourself to be called "Lord and god,", dominus et deus. Elaborate imperial ceremonial, establishing a distance between Emperor and subject that can be crossed only with the assistance of your court servants, in emulation of the Persians. Greet visitors in immense reception halls, where your elevated throne towers above all else. The minions must be required to offer you, the Emperor, their obeisance in a low bow. Only the most eminent must be permitted to kiss your bejeweled sandal."

Diocletian finally made up his mind. He would follow King Narsus" advice.

After Narsus took an oath of never fighting against Rome again, he was allowed to continue to rule in his own land. He was given a Roman escort to protect him on his way back to Persia. Many Generals were surprised of the leniency of Diocletian towards the barbarian king. Narsus had always been an enemy of Rome. There was no guarantee that he would change. He could pose problems again in the future. Why was Diocletian doing this?

To their dismay, they soon found out something even more despicable. When they were invited for a visit to his palace, they were told the new rules of behavior in the Emperor's court. They were all stunned and disappointed at Diocletian's flimsy decision to organize his court based on the Persian model. It was as if the Persian King had won the war and changed the way it was ruled.

***

After the Persian victory, a period of peace prevailed. Diocletian had ruled for more than 2 decades and was no longer young. He found himself with no military campaign to lead, and he did not want plan one.

His son-in-law Galerius moved back to Salonica, to live as the Emperor of Illyria, in the shadow of an arch he had erected for his own success and prestige by the victory over Narses, since Constantine was technically still under his command when that battle happened.

Diocletian focused his efforts on the economy of the Empire. He had discussed his plan with Galerius and he had been supportive of his idea to recalibrate the relative value of the coinage and to fix prices for essential goods and services.

Galerius had even come up with some specific changes.

"We also need to issue an edict that doubles the value of the high-grade silver coin, the argentus, from 50 to 100 copper coins, denarii. Thus the purchasing power of the state, which collects taxes in silver, is instantly doubled. Then we impose maximum prices to control inflation. The prices of more than thirty items, including wheat, barley, lentils, and beans, should be fixed according to the measure employed by military quartermasters: the army modius. That amount can feed an eight man unit, for one day, providing about a dry litre per person. Thus a camel-driver, mule-driver or ass-driver was to be paid no more than 25-60 denarii a day, whereas a shipwright for seagoing vessels might command 60 denarii. 150 denarii can buy a soldier one whole hare. Our soldiers are becoming a bit too chubby. This will keep them in shape," said Galerius.

Diocletian approved. He issued an edict and ordered the implementation of the changes.

But his reforms, the recalibration of the value of the coinage and price fixing for essential goods and services backfired. He could not control inflation. Things got worse, instead of getting better.

Diocletian tried everything to improve the economy. He undertook protracted trips through Egypt and Syria, the Empire's bread basket, in 301 and 302. His adopted son, Constantine rode beside him, ready to protect him from any possible attacks.

Unable to tame the economy, Diocletian decided to return to his Palace in Nikomedia.

There was nothing else to do for Diocletian but to turn his controlling urges to the Empire's moral and spiritual health, promoting a return to traditional Roman values, to divert people's attention from problems with the economy.

Diocletian decided to invite his son-in-law, Emperor Galerius for a visit.

When the Augustus and the Emperor of Illyria met, Diocletian was surprised to see that Galerius looked dejected.

"What's wrong?" asked Diocletian.

"I recently visited Salona, our city and new capital in Illyria. My mother is a pagan priestess, as you know, and she has built a pagan temple very close to your beautiful Palace over there. She used to have a thriving business. But because of the spread of Christianity in Illyria recently, she has lost a lot of followers. She keeps complaining to me day and night about this. She has lost her business because Illyrians are all becoming Christians in large numbers. That is not good."

"Well, such is life." said Diocletian. "At times business is good, at times bad! If Illyrians want to become Christians, there's not much that can be done about it. We have persecuted them time after time, but persecution has not worked. On the contrary."

"That's true. That's what I thought about it at first. But then after more consideration and reflection an idea came to me how to solve the problem. Because we need to solve this problem, not just for my mother, but for the entire Roman Empire as well."

"Really? You have a solution? Tell me," said Diocletian.

"The people of Rome have been worshipping pagan gods since its conception just as us, the people of Illyria. Romans got their gods from the Greeks who in turn got their gods from the Pelasgians, our forefathers. And now that we Illyrians rule the Roman Empire, we need to go back to the faith of Pelasgians, our forefathers, and restore the glory of our ancestors," said Galerius.

"I"m already intrigued," said Diocletian.

"Going back to the gods of Pelasgians will bring us unity. Illyria is currently the key to the success of Rome. It is the area where most recruited soldiers come from. The soldiers go in all the quarters of the Roman Empire. Because they are becoming Christians in large numbers, they are spreading Christianity. This is the big problem," said Galerius.

"That's true. Christians are bringing to the Roman Empire a faith that derives from another people, the people of Israel, and this faith is not Pelasgian, Greek, or Roman," Diocletian said.

"Exactly. They worship a God who they say, has created man in his image, whereas in our Pelesgian faith, we worship Gods and Goddesses who are created in man's image, in our image," Galerius said.

"But it's very difficult to decide one way or another. It's like deciding which comes first, the chicken or the egg?" said Diocletian.

"In a sense, yes. But in our Pelasgian faith, we can control gods and know how to manipulate them. But with the Christian God it's different. He is foreign, sovereign and cannot be manipulated. So having the Christian god destroys unity in our Empire. We need to ban Christianity altogether," Galerius said.

"There is a fly in the ointment though. We have been tolerant to a lot of religions. I do not see why we should not be tolerant towards Christians, even though personally I don't have a high regard for them. This is not the first time you have been talking to me about this. We have even carried out some severe local persecutions. They did not work as well as we thought they would. What's another persecution going to change? Why do you think it is going to be different this time?" asked Diocletian.

"I know, local persecutions did not work. But a big general persecution is a completely different thing. We need a persecution that has never been seen before. It will destroy all Christianity. It's better to destroy Christianity than let Christianity destroy our Empire. And when we do, we will prove that the pagan gods are the true gods. And we will keep our gods. And our priests will worship these gods. Why keep the God of the Israelites when we do not know how to control or manipulate him?" said Galerius.

"What if the Christian God is the true God? Aren"t you afraid of that," asked Diocletian.

"Well, there is a way to find out if the Christian God is the true one. Let's try this total, universal persecution," said Galerius.

"Total, universal persecution?" Diocletian asked rhetorically, totally absorbed in this ingenious idea. "I had never thought about that. I have had so many complaints about Christians. I have thought a lot about this issue. But I could not come up with a way to solve this problem. Your proposal is a great idea. Let's put the Christian God to the test!" he added with excitement.

As soon as he said these words, Constantine happened to enter the room. He came to tell Diocletian that the Praetorians were waiting for him to start their training session and were waiting for him to come and keep a watch.

"Constantine, my great General, my adopted son, before we do that, give us your view," said Diocletian.

"My view on what, Emperor Diocletian?" Constantine asked.

"We want your opinion General Constantine on a very important decision. We want to make a test. We want to test if the Christian God is true or not," said Diocletian.

"You want to put the Christian God to the test. How are you going to do that Emperor Diocletian?" asked Constantine.

"We are going to persecute his followers, the Christians," said Diocletian as Galerius nodded his head.

Constantine raised his eyebrows and looked at both of them incredulously. But they were dead serious in what they were suggesting. Cold shivers went down Constantine's spine. He immediately thought about his Christian wife Minervina.

"Persecute them? Why? They have done nothing against you Emperors. They are the best citizens you have. They respect all your decisions in all fields of governing, for as long as you allow them to follow their God. Their teaching also says, give to Ceasar what belongs to Ceasar and to God what belongs to God."

'still there is the problem I am afraid. By worshipping a god that is not a Pelasgian, Greek or Roman god, they are creating disunity in our Empire. We don't want that. We want unity in our Empire," said Diocletian.

"There has not been unity in the Roman Empire for a long time. It's not the fault of Christians. We tolerate a lot of religions Diocletian. Rome was built on the idea of liberty, even religious liberty. And in addition to this, they are Roman citizens. It would be against the law to persecute them, to imprison and harm them, without a fair trial," said Constantine.

"You've got a point there Constantine. I guess we would have to issue an edict about this Diocletian. We do not want to give the impression to the Roman citizens that we do not care about the rule of law," said Galerius.

"That sounds like a good idea to me too. I couldn't have come up with a better idea myself. So, let's make an edict to make the worship of pagan gods obligatory to everybody, to the citizens and to the soldiers," said Diocletian.

"I am sure that our Pelasgian gods will make it clear to the Christian God that they are true and he is not. This won't take long. Let's persecute Christians for a while. We will soon see that all of them will be worshipping pagan gods again, and in this way our Empire will be strong and united again," said Galerius.

Constantine's countenance became pale. He was feeling terrible. Diocletian noticed.

"Don't feel so bad about this Constantine. The idea for this persecution came from Galerius. If the God of the Christians is true and fair and just, he will punish Galerius, not you and me," said Diocletian with a grin in his face.

"But Christians have done nothing wrong, I assure you Diocletian. If you issue an edict about this, you know that it's ultimately your decision as Senior Emperor and it's you who will be remembered in history for this persecution," said Constantine.

"I don't know why you are so concerned Constantine. I am sure that the name "Christian" will be extinguished after this and there is nothing to worry about. All I will be remembered for will be something like this. "Diocletian, our great Emperor, defended the true Pelasgian gods against the false Christian God and achieved unity in the pagan Roman Empire. Ave Diocletian forever and ever"."

Constantine paused understanding that there was not much he could do. He just felt he should talk to his wife Minervina about this as soon as he returned home. He respectfully asked permission to leave the training session that day. Diocletian did not mind.

Galerius seemed satisfied with what he had achieved. He knew how Christians were going to react to the edict. They would refuse to obey. This would just point them out. And then all hell would be let loose. Christians would be thrown to lions as food. Many of them would be killed by the sword. Others would be hanged in wooden crosses. Galerius rubbed his hands.

***

On his way home, Constantine felt that things were getting completely out of control. For some reason he had always felt proud of the Roman Empire in the past. When he had heard stories how Paul, the Christian Apostle had been in circumstances where he could have been tortured by some praetorian soldiers, he had told them that he was a Roman citizen, and just that had made the soldiers stop and send him to trial.

Now it seemed that the Roman Emperor himself was about to change something so good about the Roman Empire. The individual rights of its citizens. Constantine was hoping in his heart that something would happen to stop the course of these developments in the Roman Empire but things seemed to be heading in the wrong direction regardless of his wishes.

When he told Minervina about what he had heard from Diocletian, Minervina became very concerned. Constantine was surprised to see the extremely pale look in Minervina's face.

"What's wrong sweetheart?" Constantine asked her.

"There's no doubt in my mind that Diocletion is going to kill many Christians," she said.

The definite manner in which Minervina said those words surprised Constantine even more.

"It's not for sure. This probably means that the Emperor is going to make things a bit more difficult for Christians," Constantine said.

"Things are going to get a lot worse Constantine. Many Christians will lose their lives. I can't even exclude myself. For this reason, I want you to promise me one thing," Minervina said.

"Don't be silly. You are overreacting Minervina. There is no danger to you. You are my wife," Constantine said.

"Promise me that even if something happens to me, you will not take any revenge," Minervina said and looked straight into Constantine's eyes.

"You are being completely irrational now. Nothing is going to happen to you," Constantine said.

"Promise me that you will not keep revenge in your heart, that you will forgive and forget. Even if I die, I am going to a better place. It's God's will. Promise me that you will not take any revenge. I insist," Minervina said.

Constantine's eyeballs became bigger. He looked at Minervina steadfastly. She was dead serious. "Promise," said Constantine.

"That's all I wanted to hear," said Minervina, leaving Constantine perplexed in his thoughts.

***

The edict of persecution soon became a reality after it was signed into law by Diocletian. Ordinary people and soldiers now had to offer libations to the pagan gods regularly. Diocletian's first universal and most vicious persecution to stamp out Christianity started in his own hometown Salona, just above Shkodra, the administrative seat of the province of Illyria. Even in Nicomedia, the administrative seat of the East, persecution of Christians spread fast. Many pagan citizens found this edict not to intervene with their beliefs and they gladly obeyed their Emperor.

But for Christians this was a tough test of their faith. They were in a great dilemma. They wanted to obey their Emperor, but the teaching of the Bible was clear about questions that did not have to do with the secular life, but with God. Any edict against their God had to be disobeyed. They could not betray their God to obey somebody who claimed to be a god. They could not worship false gods. They had to disobey, because they loved their God and were ready to do anything for him and they loved their religious freedom. How could they offer libations to other gods besides worshiping their God. That would be religious syncretism, worshiping true and false gods at the same time. That could lead believers to abandon the true faith. Diocletian had to be disobeyed. Constantine was walking around amidst soldiers on a Sunday afternoon, time when everybody was supposed to offer libations to the pagan gods. Generals were no exception. Generals and soldiers, all of them had to obey. Constantine had never in his young life decided if it was God who created man or man who created God. He knew that it was one way or the other, but he had not considered the question deeply and carefully enough to decide firmly one way or the other. He had never found the truth. Maybe because this truth seemed unfathomable and he had to wait until the truth somehow became known to him. And he really wanted to know in his heart of hearts if the Christian God or the Pelasgian gods were true.

So together with many other generals and soldiers, Constantine obeyed the edict and mechanically went through the motions of throwing wheat on some fire that Sunday afternoon. But right after him, a Christian by the name of Mark, took out a cross and told his superiors that he was a Christian and could not offer libations to pagan gods. Mark was arrested immediately and tortured on the spot. The officers were trying to force him to change his mind, but Mark was resolute.

Constantine was stunned. What made Mark so faithful to his Christian faith and God? Constantine thought about this as the soldiers took Mark away to send him to prison. Could it be that the Christian God was the only true God out there for Mark. Persecution had started in all its severity. Would it show the result one way or another?

It seemed strange that this persecution was happening in Nikomedia, alongside other provincial towns and cities, especially in Illyricum, where Galerius had a great influence as its Emperor. Constantine felt sorry that things were taking such a terrible turn. He wished he could do something, find a solution or a way to stop all this madness. But he felt powerless over and over.

He knew that more soldiers would be arrested and tortured and even killed because he knew that many of them were Christians.

And that was exactly what happened. Scenes of Christians getting dragged in the streets of Nikomedia, getting tortured, and sometimes stabbed in the back, became a daily occurrence. People who hated their neighbors because they were of a different ethnicity or race would often accuse them as Christians, just to put them in trouble. The soldiers did not wait for things to go to a judge. The strict Roman law was clear on this. "If you are accused, you are guilty, until proven innocent." The soldiers had their orders. They were the judges and did whatever they saw fit in their eyes. They asked for money or other valuables to release the detained. Corruption flourished. If they could not get money, they would scar Christians in their face, making scars in the shape of a cross, so people would recognize them and ostracize them.

Chaos started to dominate life in Nikomedia. The more persecution increased, the more Diocletian desired to believe that it was the fault of the Christians why the Roman Empire had become poor and had no unity, even though deep down inside he knew that this was not true. But he did not want to believe it was his own fault either. He felt he was doing all he could.

Under Galerius" pressure, Diocletian decided to give a clear example of how far he was willing to go to break the will of Christians. Accompanied by some praetorians, Galerius was given permission to blind a Christian in the city square where a meeting was already taking place.

In it, a Roman tax-collector was trying to collect money from people, standing in front of some wealthy and poor people and talking to them.

"You all know how the barbarians have ravaged many villages and have treated many people cruelly. They continue to be a great danger on all sides of the Roman Empire. It is essential that we stop them. At present the Court of Diocletian does not have enough money. So we need your support, to pay for our soldiers, who will continue to fight continuously to defend our borders and bring all those who attack us under subjection. We need more money."

"But we don't have any more money for the Government," said someone from the crowd. "We have already paid our taxes. We are broke."

"Diocletian wants money because he is greedy. We don't have any money," another in the crowd shouted.

As soon as he noticed Galerius and the praetorians, the Roman tax-collector made a sign for people to keep order.

Galerius then took the center stage and started speaking.

"It is Diocletian's belief that Christians are to blame for the problems of our Empire, for our poverty and disunity. So we are going to set an example of what will happen to Christians if they do not offer libations to Pagan gods and if you do not support his policies to address these problems."

Some merchants, openly defiant, hissed at him and said: "That is a lie, a big lie!"

Galerius kept his cool and continued talking.

"This is what is going to happen to those who disobey Diocletian. This is just an example. This man you see here," and he pointed at Mark, "is a soldier who did not offer libations. We are going to blind him today and you are going to witness this event now. I hope you will learn some lessons from this."

Then the praetorians brought Mark to the center area. He was laid flat on the ground, facing the sky. The executioner brought the hot branding iron near to his face. As the red hot iron touched his eyes, Mark started to howl and groan for a few moments. Then he fainted. The whole crowd fell silent too. Then a soldier took out a knife and with its tip, carved out a cross on Mark's forehead.

This incident soon became known throughout the town. Many started to worry about these developments. Most of the wealthy people decided to pay more taxes after this.

Diocletian thought that most Christians, if not all of them, would yield after the hard measures he had taken. But they did not. They preferred to get arrested or tortured or even killed than deny their faith in their one true God.

But problems kept increasing. More famine, lack of food and other essentials, more decease and more wounded soldiers were seen in Nikomedia as days passed by. And then out of the blue, there was a big fire in Diocletian's palace. Galerius exploited the opportunity to blame the Christians as the arsonists. Meantime, people were saying that it was Galerius himself who started the fire.

Suspecting it was started by Christians, as Galerius suggested, Diocletian decided to go to more extreme measures. He gave his soldiers orders to go to the new church of Nikomedia, the one in front of his palace, and kill anybody they found in the church.

As people of all ages went to church of Nikomedia to worship their God, their service was interrupted by the shouts of soldiers entering with their drawn swords in hand and shouting "Praise pagan gods!"

Everybody turned their heads and looked at the soldiers with great surprise in their face.

Then Lactantius, the pastor of the church spoke.

"We worship only one God, Father, Son, and Holy Spirit" he said from the pulpit.

Some soldiers started to approach the pulpit. The preacher stood there fearless. Members of the congregation in the front stood up and created a dividing wall between Lactantius and the Roman soldiers.

"Say praise Jupiter or we will kill you right now," shouted the commander of the soldiers to Lactantius.

"Praise Jesus Christ, my Lord and Savior. This is my only answer," said the preacher.

This enraged Diocletian's soldiers. Their commander suddenly killed one of the people among those who had formed the human wall.

An outcry was heard from all the people in the church and then a silence followed. One could hear a needle drop."

"Who among you people here wants to praise Jesus?" asked the commander of the soldiers hoping that all would be afraid of him now.

"I do," said one old man.

"I do," said one woman.

"I do," said a little kid.

"I do," said the whole congregation in one voice.

The soldiers lost their heads completely. And then the turmoil started.

"Kill them all," said their commander.

Like jackals attacking lambs, the soldiers began killing Christians. The terrified children and women began crying out loud with a cry that makes any heart break in two. But the soldier's heart was made of stone. They did not care and killed indiscriminately whomever they could. The slaughter was immense.

As the number of Christians in the church was in the hundreds, a great number rushed to the door and managed to escape, even though many were wounded in the process.

The Christians did everything to defend themselves. They fought against the soldiers with everything they could. But the soldiers were trained and armed and it was impossible to win against them.

The floor of the church was now stained with blood in many places. Some people even slipped on it as they were moving without paying any attention to the floor. The bloodbath was horrendous.

Despite the great bloodshed, many Christians managed to escape, saving their pastor, Lactantius, as well.

When Diocletian received the report of the bloodshed in the church by his commander, he felt satisfied that many believers had been killed on the spot. He was surprised though that Lactantius, the pastor, had escaped. But what perplexed him more was the fact that he still could not understand why the Christians had chosen to stay faithful to the Christian God and not return to worship the Roman pagan gods. But such was their decision. And they paid with their lives for disobeying his edict.

"I have seen strange things in my life," said Galerius to Diocletian, "but this is the strangest of them all. They did not deny their faith, even though they knew very well that they were going to get killed for this," said Galerius.

"I am glad our soldiers killed many of the Christians. They are more foreign to me than any foreigner I have met," said Diocletian.

"But our job is not done yet. Let's raze the church building to the ground. Jesus Christ always complained that he had no house for himself when he was on earth, I have heard. Well, it seems that he will have to be homeless again!"

"So be it," said Diocletian.

Galerius wasted no time. Putting himself at the head of a special unit, he rode towards the church.

The special unit surrounded the church. They had axes and hammers instead of swords and spears. In a few hours they brought the whole building down. The building turned into a pile of wood and stones and dust and debris.

Happy with what he had achieved, Galerius returned to the imperial palace.

"Just as I said. Jesus Christ is homeless again," a happy Galerius told Diocletian.

"I watched from the window of my palace as soldiers brought the church building down. When it turned into rubble, I rubbed my hands and said to my wife. "The Church is gone now. I cannot see it anymore. Where is their God?""

"Maybe he is dead," joked Galerius. "I need to destroy and burn a few more churches and see if their God will become alive," he added, and with that, he asked permission to leave.

Diocletian nodded. As soon as Galerius left, Diocletian felt a sharp pain in his chest. He sank into a chair grasping for air.

When his wife Prisca entered the room, Diocletian had collapsed on the floor. He tried to hide his pain, but failed.

"You are not feeling well, my Emperor," Prisca said helping him to get up. "Maybe I should call the doctor."

Diocletian wanted to say no but the pain was too sharp and he almost fainted. They both walked towards the Emperor's bed.

After Diocletian lay down, Prisca ordered the guard to call the doctor. She herself hurried to get some camomile tea, hoping that it would help him to fall asleep.

***

Diocletian's health did not improve much despite the care provided by the doctor. The news that he was sick spread very quickly. The generals heard about it from the palace guards.

Galerius did everything to seize this golden opportunity. And now that Diocletian was sick, this dream seemed easier to be fulfilled. He had a good chance to win his father-in-law's trust and good favor and become Senior Emperor instead of Diocletian.

The generals were visiting Diocletian whenever they could and all were telling him to retire, so he could pay more attention to his health. Diocletian was hoping he would get well soon but he did not recover completely and in the end decided to listen to his generals.

Galerius decided to ask Diocletian to promote him as Emperor when Diocletian would leave. He knew very well that Diocletian had groomed Constantine to become Emperor in the future. Constantine had excelled as a general and all the soldiers had great respect for him. Constantine was number one in Diocletian's list.

But things could be changed.

Constantine had not supported Diocletian's persecution of the Christians at all. Everyone had noticed that. He had avoided all duty when he had been asked to persecute Christians. This could be held against him now that Diocletian hated Christians so much, especially after his Palace was set on fire.

Diocletian's judgment had also been affected by his sickness. He was not able to make good decisions any longer. That was true even before he was sick. That was the very reason why he allowed the persecution of Christians in the first place. He also wanted to retire. Soldiers did not trust he could make good decisions and in the hour of the battle, where it was a matter of life or death, bad decisions often spelt death. And no soldier wanted that.

Galerius brought the issue up when he visited Diocletian. He decided to act fast because he dreaded the inevitable stroke of death. He also knew that Diocletian had began to consider the question of his successor seriously.

Diocletian did not hide the fact that he was thinking of choosing Constantine as his successor because Constantine was of Illyrian origin just as himself, of illustrious descent, good-looking, of profound intellect, courageous in battle, young, and above all akin to Emperor Constantius by race.

"In preference to all others I am thinking of leaving him as successor to the Empire, giving him the reign of power," Diocletian said.

"You have been ill-advised Diocletian. As your son-in-law, I can ensure the best rule of the Empire," Galerius said.

Diocletian's wife, the empress as well, talked to him and said that Galerius would be the best choice because he was married to their daughter Valeria.

Diocletian was not sure if he was ready to step down as well. He wanted to continue to rule for some time to come, but Galerius again insisted.

"Emperor, we do not behold you in the same health as heretofore, but you seem worried and obsessed by unbearable thoughts and without the courage to fight anybody. You also have not started any new campaign in a long time. It is time for you to live a quiet life at home and forget about the sorrows that ruling an Empire brings and more that are in store in the future," Galerius told him.

After this Galerius and Prisca stood aloof and added no more words, but with eyes cast down and both hands covered, stood a minute plunged in thought and then made their usual obeisance and left his room.

The next day they came again to talk to Diocletian, and seeing that he looked at them more cheerfully than the day before, they both went close up to him.

"You are our Emperor. I am your most devoted slave, ready to die, if need be, for you. And do not let any consideration unnerve you and lead you to indecision," Galerius told Diocletian.

Upon these words he gave the Emperor an oath and Galerius and Prisca were able to guess the choice that Diocletian would make despite the fact that he did not express his opinion. Straightway Galerius associated himself still more closely with the Emperor and making his good intentions clear to him by many proofs he promised he would bravely assist him in any undertaking to which Diocletian would summon him, even after he would step down.

The empress reminded Diocletian that Galerius was from the same stock as he was. He was Illyrian too. And she told him that Galerius would not consider Constantine as a rival after reaching the throne, but he would regard him as a friend. Constantine would not be ousted from the Empire.

The Emperor seemed more and more agreeing with what Galerius and the empress were telling him.

Diocletian understood that Galerius and the empress were scheming to get Constantine out of their way. But because all his army knew that he was grooming Constantine to become Emperor, he had to take precautions of not disappointing them to the point of revolt. That was why it was hard for him to decide.

"The soldiers want Constantine as Emperor," Diocletian told Galerius.

Galerius reminded Diocletian of the stance of Constantine towards Christians.

"You cannot promote Constantine, Emperor. He is completely different from you. He supports Christians. He will change everything, all your policies. You can bet on that. And if he and his family do not go down, and he comes to power, then it's me and your daughter and my family who will go down. We will get destroyed. Why should my family go down. On the contrary, Constantine and his family must go down. Do not promote him. Promote me," Galerius said.

Diocletian stood pensive for a moment, looking at Galerius. "Galerius is right," Diocletian thought to himself. "Constantine will change everything in the Roman Empire."

Diocletian thought if he could trust Galerius. His reasoning was persuasive. Constantine had shown support for Christians. Diocletian could not put up with that. His heart was filled with anger and he made up his mind. He nodded to Galerius. He had let himself be persuaded by the entreaties of his son-in-law. The old man failed to see that he was arranging matters in a way which was not only unjust to Constantine, but also disastrous for the Roman Empire.

"You are right Galerius. Constantine must go down."

Diocletian was actually surprised that he felt good and happy about fulfilling Galerius" request. Galerius had to become Emperor if he wanted a great future for him and his daughter. And he knew that Galerius would not support Christians. Whereas Constantine and his family had to go to oblivion.

Diocletian thought more about this but his decision seemed right.

Constantine had brought all this on himself. His stance towards his edict had left a bad impression on him. And moreover, Constantine's wife was a Christian, too. And Constantine was just an adopted son, not his biological son.

So Diocletian made up his mind. Constantine's family had to be destroyed.

The scheme of the death of Constantine and Minervina was planned out carefully by Galerius. Minervina was to be killed by poison. And Constantine was to be sent in the thick of the battle and there left to be killed. Their son Crispus would be killed too.

The scheme was kept as an imperial secret. Only a few people knew about it. Just Galerius, Diocletian and some of his servants.

Prisca, Diocletian's wife, was not in the know about the scheme, but she would be the main instrument to be used in this plot.

Prisca invited Minervina to her palace for tea.

Minervina accepted the invitation after she talked to Constantine's mother Helen about it.

Minervina showed up in time, about 5 in the evening. She was cheerful and grateful for having been invited and expressed her thanks to Prisca. Prisca also was glad to see Minervina. They sat in two sofas in the waiting room while Athena, Prisca's Greek servant woman brought them tea and biscuits. She had put poison in Minervina's tea.

Prisca and Minervina started chatting courteously for a few moments.

Prisca asked Minervina about her son.

"Oh, he is doing great. I left him with his grandma Helen. God has blessed me with a son like him. He is cheerful and likes to play and imitate Constantine, in what he says and does. He is my pride and joy."

"Like father, like son. I am sure he will grow up to become a brave man like his father," said Prisca.

Athena was standing up in a corner of the room listening to what both ladies were saying and looking at them, waiting for Minervina to start drinking her poisoned tea, which would kill her fast. As soon as the ladies started to drink their tea, Minervina started to convulse heavily.

Athena immediately left the room to go to talk to the doctor who would come in and declare the cause of death as heart-attack.

When both she and the doctor entered the room, Minervina was lying lifeless on her coach. The doctor checked her pulse and declared her dead.

"It was a heart attack" he announced with fake pity in his face.

As Diocletian could not trust Athena to keep the secret he had arranged for her murder too. As soon as Athena left for her home, she was stabbed to death by a soldier and her body was put in a cart and dumped into an open grave in the graveyard.

**

The news of the death of Minervina came as lightening in a sunny day to Constantine. This was a clear sign that things were out of control. He did not know exactly what to think and what to do. He suspected foul play even though he had no proof. His heart was filled with rage and he wanted to find the person to direct this rage to. He felt he had to do something. So he went to see the doctor.

The doctor assured him and his mother Helen that Minervina had had a heart attack and nothing could have been done about it.

His teacher Lactantius came to console them too. Her death was the will of God, he said. This reminded Constantine of the promise he had given to Minervina. He would not seek revenge.

Helen and Constantine accepted this death with dignity and an enduring heart. They organized Minervina's funeral as best as they could, and paid their last respects.

Constantine was devastated. He had lost the love of his life and did not know how to deal with this misfortune in other ways but to try to take care of their son Crispus and to get closer to the Christian God in whom Minervina had believed so much. He spent much time with his Christian teacher, Lactantius with whom he forged a sincere friendship. The pain Constantine felt was immense. His pain could be relieved only by the words of Lactantius that Minervina was now in a better place, with her heavenly Father, the God of the living, as she had hoped and believed. Even though Constantine still did not have complete faith in heaven, he sincerely wished things were that way. There was no other way to deal with such a pain.

He and all other generals had been informed that Diocletian was going to make a decision on a Sunday afternoon at his Palace. They all had to be there for this meeting.

***

All the great generals and captains showed up in Diocletian's Palace in time. The great majority of them were already convinced that Diocletian would choose Constantine as Caesar of Illyricum, who clearly would later become his next successor. Constantine's person radiated strength and dignity and an unapproachable majesty, like a true eagle, all qualities of a great Emperor.

When they saw Constantine in the group of generals who were accompanying Diocletian to the stage, they thought that their presentiment was right.

Then Diocletian started speaking to the crowd of generals and captains.

"An Emperor is like a lion leading other lions in the heat of battle. He must be strong to provide for many and defend his own from danger. He must know how to lead the Empire and unite the Empire. People must like him and he must like people. And people must accept his leadership. A leader must have strength, courage and other martial qualities, and be good in politics, diplomacy or unification," Diocletian said.

Diocletian continued to talk and the speech seemed too long to the soldiers and generals but everything Diocletian said seemed to fit perfectly with the qualities of Constantine, and so they waited patiently for the moment when Diocletian would choose him as a successor.

But that did not happen. When Diocletian mentioned the name of Galerius as his successor, a depreciative sigh was heard among the people. They looked at each other in disbelief. The disappointment was overwhelming to many of them. Constantine did not talk. It was as if he knew that this was going to happen.

Galerius walked to the center stage all puffed up and started talking.

He praised the decision of Diocletian to elect him as an Emperor.

He said he understood that some of the generals and captains were unhappy that Constantine had not been chosen but he promised that he would keep Constantine close as one of his greatest generals, just as Diocletian had done in the past. Constantine's father after all was in charge of the western part of the Empire, of Britain, Gaul and Spain, and he wanted good relations with other Emperors. And Constantine could one day become Emperor of that part of the Empire. A note of cooperation would be sent to Constantius about these late developments as well.

This seemed to pacify the crowd to a degree. But some unhappiness continued to linger.

\#

CHAPTER 3

CONSTANTINE REUNITES WITH HIS FATHER, CONSTANTIUS

WHEN CONSTANTIUS, Constantine's father, heard about the unusual events which had happened in Nikomedia, Minervina's death and the fact that Constantine had not been chosen as Emperor, he began to worry. Diocletian had adopted Constantine exactly for that reason. He had no sons of his own and needed someone to take his place when he would be gone. The fact that it did not happen made him thing that something suspicious was going on in the east.

Constantius began to worry even more when he himself fell sick and needed help. His sickness advanced fast. He could not explain clearly why things were going that way but he felt that they were going in the wrong direction and he had to do something to change the course of events and, above all, to protect his son's life. He had strong premonitions that Galerius wanted to kill Constantine. There had been many examples in the past when sons of Emperors had been the target of the jealousy of Emperors. He judged that such was the case this time.

Besides this, he also needed help for himself more than ever. He needed to have his son Constantine fighting by his side because he was suffering from a decease and he was not sure how long he would live. He wanted his son to be there for him.

Constantius sat down and wrote a letter to Galerius requesting that Constantine be sent to his service as he desperately needed help because he was sick. He needed a strong reliable general by his side. And who could be better than his son.

Galerius was not willing to let Constantine go. He replied that he needed Constantine's services too and he could not help in this case. And so Constantious's request was rejected. This just increased Constantius' anxiety.

Galerius could not wait for the right opportunity to have Constantine eliminated. He was like a wolf looking for his pray. He was still afraid that because of the popularity that Constantine had among the soldiers, they could attempt to make him Emperor by killing him, Galerius. This had been a normal thing in the Roman Empire lately. Many of the last Emperors had been great generals who with the support of their soldiers had captured the throne. In fact, becoming a barrack's Emperor was normal.

But killing Constantine was not an easy task. He was a man of no equal strength. Also ganging up on him could not work. In fact, it was very difficult to find trusted soldiers to plan and carry the attack in complete secrecy. Most of the soldiers respected Constantine, and the conspiracy would very likely be discovered before it was carried out. And then it was the problem of his biological father, Constantius, the Emperor of the west. He could retaliate by starting a civil war. So open action seemed out of the question.

The only option for Galerius remained the secret way. So he decided to go with what he had thought previously. In the heat of battle, he would give orders to soldiers to retreat and since Constantine was always in the first line, he would be most exposed.

On the next battle against a large army of barbarians, a clan of Goths, he saw the window of opportunity he was looking for.

Constantine was sent in the thickest of the battle. As the battle raged, Galerius gave an order to his soldiers to retreat. Confusion filled the ranks of the Romans.

Galerius was sure his plan would work because he knew that Constantine would be among the last to retreat. His chances of survival were close to zero.

As the Roman soldiers began to retreat, Constantine knew he had to act fast. The retreat order did not make sense to him. The enemy troops were more numerous but the Romans were winning. In a loud voice, Constantine told the soldiers to stay. Galerius was stunned.

Soldier obeyed Constantine. They knew that they were going to lose the battle and their lives if they retreated and they listened to Constantine's words 'stay and we win. Leave and we all die. Courage soldiers, courage!" And so they stayed.

They fought with Constantine. They trusted him. They knew that his judgment was sharpest when the situation was the direst. He had always been victorious. Soldiers called him "Always Victorious". He had not failed them ever. Not even once. He was their true leader in battle and nobody else.

And that day Constantine was like a tornado. Wherever he attacked the Goths, it was as if the eye of the storm was ferociously destroying everything. Soldiers were flying off their horses one after another. Heads were being severed.

Following his example, Constantine's friends became more courageous and fought with even more force and energy.

When they subdued the enemy and brought many of them as captives, Galerius pretended he was happy. But inside, he was kicking himself for having lost his golden opportunity to have Constantine killed.

***

Constantine became more pensive after this battle. The order of Galerius to retreat had come at the worst moment and the Roman army could have lost and many people would have died. He knew that Galerius was a skilled general and he did not think that he could have made this mistake accidentally. Things could have gone terribly wrong had not soldiers listened to his advice to stand strong and not retreat. He felt that Galerius was planning something against him personally and he needed to do something about it. He knew that he needed to act fast. Maybe he had to go and fight for his father. And his father needed his help too because he was not feeling well lately.

As Generals were celebrating the victory over barbarians in the Imperial Palace, Constantine approached Galerius. He told him that his father Constantius was sick and needed his help and he needed Galerius permission to go to his help.

Galerius was already a little drunk but not enough as to allow Constantine to leave. Other drunk generals encouraged him to let him go. Galerius said "no" at first, adding that "Constantine's presence in Nikomedia was necessary, but the other drunk generals became even more demanding.

"Is this how you want to reward the man who saved your thick skin?" asked one of the generals.

"He did not save my skin. I was at quite a safe distance," replied Galerius.

"So what is the problem then? Are we not brave enough to protect you?" asked the general and looked at Galerius.

Galerius did not answer.

"You have us. Don't you trust us? You have nothing to fear. You have to let him go!"

When the general mentioned fear, Galerius knew that if he continued to say "no" they would get offended and they would also think he was a coward.

Finally, even though reluctantly, he said "yes".

Constantine seized the opportunity.

He went over to his house and told Helen to get Crispus and pack up a few necessary things for a long and immediate journey. Helen was surprised but she did as told.

Together with a small guard of Illyrian knights, his Latin and Christian Bishop, Lactantius, Constantine and Helen and Crispus got on a coach and started their ride towards Bolougne, where Constantius was staying. The small group moved at a fast pace. There was not much conversation going on between them. All that could be heard was the sound of horse hoofs hitting the ground at regular intervals.

After a long and tiring trip, Constantine and his escort reached Bulougne.

The meeting of Constantine and his father was a cordial one but Constantius was ill. Never had the Emperor of the West suffered so severely from a sharp pain in his lungs.

This situation had started years ago, at first for intervals but now it did not come periodically. It was continuous and the irritation unending and he was bleeding blood when he coughed.

When Constantine arrived, Constantius was anxious to get his son acquainted with all of his trusted generals and men and he immediately introduced him to them. And as Constantine was a sincere person, he made friends with the generals and other people quickly.

But the poor health of his father caused him great concerns and they spent a lot of time together. When the Caesar was having a good day, he would go for a ride in the forest with Constantine and a few soldiers, hunting. The soldiers were doing all the hunting while the Caesar just watched and talked to Constantine. Constantius explained how things had turned out for him. They both wanted to catch up and find all about what had happened in the past to them.

"Immediately upon my elevation as Caesar, I was assigned the task of crushing Carausius. In 293, I drove the rebel out of north-western Gaul, to Britain. This was no easy job, as Carausius had widespread support and wealth at his disposal. He was the only man claiming the title Emperor who at that time was able to mint coins in silver. These coins expressed his claim to rule alongside Diocletian and Maximian, whose heads were shown behind his own," Constantius said.

"So how did you win against him?" asked Constantine.

"Carausius was betrayed by his own. He was killed by his deputy, Allectus. Then I turned to the Rhine frontier, before settling affairs with Allectus in 296. The initial victory was won by my Praetorian Prefect, Ascleiodotus. I arrived triumphantly at London. I even minted a coin which depicts a woman, representing the city of London, kneeling before me, the Emperor, a mounted warrior, as a sign of submission to my rule. I shared my success with three of my colleagues, and all took the cognomen, Britannicus Maximus," the Caesar said.

Constantius was glad to find out now that Constantine was a mature adult and could judge things better than he had thought at first. Constantine was glad too that his real father, Constantius was indeed a more compassionate man and leader than Diocletian. He told the Caesar so.

"You're a better leader than Diocletian, father," Constantine said and added, "I lost my respect for Diocletian when he issued an edict to persecute the Christians."

Constantius nodded and told Constantine that he had completely ignored that edict.

"Never seen a worse edict in my life. Never read about any worse edict either. I could not support it in any way. How could I? We cannot select a certain group of civilians in the Roman Empire and attack them. It's a great injustice. You know that my closest friends are Illyrian soldiers whose forefathers were evangelized by the Apostle Paul himself. When we have been fighting against the barbarians, Christianity is what we have tried to bring to them. In this way we thought we were helping them, trying to bring them from their savage state to one of civilization and gentleness. And we did this everywhere we went. We put the settled order of civilized life in Britain, Gaul, and Spain, regions currently under my rule, and other areas as well. And the Christian God has been faithful to us bringing us prosperity and success in most of our endeavors, if not all of them. What great ingratitude to attack Christians!" said Constantius, his eyes filled with sadness.

Constantine nodded. He told his father that his respect for Christians increased much more after the edict of persecution, and he sympathized with Christians and even though he had not yet come to believe wholeheartedly in the Christian God and he was still searching for the truth about Him. The persecution had changed his opinion about Diocletian as well.

"I have never seen more Christian blood shed without any reason or cause. There was no offense initiated by Christians. Diocletian and other leaders already knew more or less what the response of the Christians was going to be. When Diocletian and Galerius made that edict, they knew that they were giving the death sentence to Christians, and they thought this was fine. They decided to be cruel. And the most absurd thing in all of this was the fact that the persecution was initiated just because Galerius" mother, a high priest of the pagan gods, had lost her followers. What an evil edict, indeed!" Constantine said.

A feeling of indignation towards Diocletian and Galerius filled both father and son. And both agreed that they would never support such an edict, no matter what.

The bond between father and son grew. During this time of peace, Constantine got to know some other members of his family, his three half-sisters, Constantia, Anastasia and Illyriana and Constantious got to know Constantine and Crispus better.

Both Generals, father and son, had ample time to catch up with what had happened in each other's lives and it became clear to them that they could work together to keep their part of the Roman Empire in peace.

Even as they were having this good time together, a messenger came in and told Constantious that the Picts were attacking the Roman Empire.

As soon as the messenger left, Constantious told Constantine that his health was deteriorating fast and that he needed his support in his campaign against the Picts, a very strong people in Brittain.

"Definitely. Never felt more motivated to fight than besides you, father. Besides, it's never good for a soldier or general to stay idle. My wife Minervina would always remind me not to become lazy like Achilles" said Constantine.

"Thank you" said Constantius.

"Thank you for your invitation. It is an honor to serve under such a great Emperor as you, father" said Constantine, not without some pride and emotion.
#

CHAPTER 4

CONSTANTINE, THE EMPEROR OF THE WEST

IN THE FOLLOWING DAYS, father and son prepared the army which would be fighting against the Picts. Constantious told Constantine that the Picts were more dangerous than the Germans and all other barbarians. If he could win against them, he could conquer all the world. "The Picts' battle-order does not agree at all with that of the Roman Empire. For with them it's not shield upon shield, and spear against spear. The Picts right and left wing, and center are quite disconnected and the phalanxes stand as if severed from each other. Consequently if an army attacks their right or left wing, their center may swoop down upon it and all the rest of the army posted behind it, and like whirlwinds throw the opposing body into confusion. Now for their weapons of war:-they do not use spears much, but surround the enemy completely and shoot at him with arrows, and they make this defence from a distance. When a Pict pursues, he captures his man with the bow; when he is pursued he conquers with his darts; he throws a dart and the flying dart hits either the horse or its rider, and as it has been dispatched with very great force it passes right through the body; so skilled are they in the use of the bow. Having noticed this from long experience we have to arrange our lines and phalanxes in such a way that the Picts should shoot from the right side, the side on which the shields were advanced, and that our men should shoot from the left, the side on which the Picts' bodies are unprotected," Constantius said.

"Thank you father for your information. I am confident that we will find the right strategy, courage and strength to win against them. As you are not feeling well, it is not necessary for you to come and fight with us," Constantine said.

"The threat is so serious that I cannot stay back and relax" Constantious said. "My presence will be a great boost of morale for my soldiers. I have complete confidence in your abilities but the soldiers do not know you yet, and that can be a problem."

"As you wish father," said Constantine understanding that his father had never seen him lead soldiers into battle. He was happy though that he would be fighting together with his father.

A fleet of 1000 triremes got ready to sail off towards Britain.

***

The Picts' army had camped in a forest waiting for the Roman army to cross the sea. Their leader William had invited his best generals to dinner with him. They were making fun of the "sickness" of the Emperor, which they thought only a fear to fight against them. All generals laughed loudly as soon as someone mentioned the Emperor's "sickness" while they were eating their grilled meat of lamb and drinking their red wine.

Constantious knew that fighting against the Picts was not easy. They had caused troubles in the past. Now a fresh potion of troubles was brewed for him again. William was planning to devastate the Roman army again and assembled his forces from Scotland to see whether he might possibly be able to attack the Roman Emperor successfully. As the whole of the William's plan had already been reported to Constantius, he contemplated advancing as far as London with his Roman army and there forcing William into a closely contested battle. For that town was the center of all England. Therefore he had solicited troops from foreign countries as well, especially a large mercenary force from Germany, and called up his own army from all sides. But, while he was making these preparations against William in Germany, the old trouble in his lungs attacked Constantius. And his forces kept coming in from all quarters, even Gaul and Spain, but only in driblets, not all together, because their countries were so far away, and the pain prevented the Emperor not merely from carrying out his projected plan, but even from walking at all. And he was vexed at being confined to his couch not so much because of the excessive pain in his lungs, but by reason of the postponement of his expedition against the Picts to have a good size army. The barbarian William was well aware of this and consequently despoiled the whole of Britain at his leisure during this interval when the Roman Emperor was inactive and made several onslaughts upon the Romans in different places. Never before had the Emperor's army suffered so many losses. The situation was critical because he was very ill and he knew that his end was getting near.

William's followers continued to uphold that this suffering was only a pretence at illness, not really an illness, and that hesitation and indolence were disguised under the cloak of gout; and they continued to joke about it on every occasion, when eating or drinking, and as natural orators the Picts wove moral talks and satirical comedies about the Emperor's sufferings in his lungs. For they would impersonate doctors and other people busied about the Emperor and place the Emperor himself in the middle, lying on a couch, and make a play of it before the soldiers. And these puerile games aroused much laughter among the Picts.

These doings did not escape the Emperor and his son Constantine and they made both of them boil with anger and provoked them still more to war with them and finally they were able to sail off towards England. "Laughs best he who laughs last," Constantius said to Constantine. After a short interval during their voyage, Constantius was partly relieved from pain. When they reached land, things were getting even better. Constantius and his army ferried over to London, and raised camp to a wide field there, to await the arrival of his armies and the mercenary army he had engaged. When they were all assembled he moved away from there with all his forces and occupied the fort of Saint Albans, 19 miles outside London. Then after three days he returned and encamped on this side of the bridge of Thames near the fountain of Celts as it was called; for he thought best to send the army over the bridge first to pitch their tents in a suitable spot and then to cross himself by the same bridge and erect the imperial tent in company with all the army. But the wily Picts were devastating the plain lying at the close to London and on hearing of the Emperor's advance against them, they were terrified and immediately lighted a number of beacon fires, thus giving beholders the illusion of a large army. And the sky was lighted up by these fires and frightened many of the inexperienced soldiers but nothing of all this troubled the Emperor. Then the Picts collected all the booty and prisoners and went away; and at dawn the Emperor hastened after them to the plain with the desire of overtaking them on the spot, but he missed his quarry. On the contrary he found a number of Romans still breathing, and many corpses, which naturally enraged him. But he was very anxious to pursue the Picts so as not to lose all his prey, and, as it was impossible for the whole army to follow up the fugitives quickly, he pitched his palisades on the spot near Verulamium and selecting at once a detachment of brave light-armed soldiers, he entrusted them with the pursuit of the barbarians and told them which road to take after the wretches. He put his Constantine as the leader of these soldiers. This small Roman army led by Constantine overtook the Picts with all their booty and captives at a place called the Prae Hill by the natives and rushed upon them like a consuming fire and soon killed most of them but took a few alive and after collecting all the booty there they returned brilliantly victorious to the Emperor. After welcoming them and learning of the total destruction of the enemy Constantius and Constantine returned to Ebarokium, named after "barracks", called York as well, where the Emperor's Palace was situated.

When they reached it they stayed in that town because the Picts had been defeated and what was left of their army did not attack again.

The victory was celebrated by all soldiers and generals with much merriment, food and drinks. The Empress meanwhile was lodging at East York at a safe place and while there she got the news of the Emperor's victory and his return to West York. Directly the Emperor sent the imperial galley to fetch her, firstly because he was always dreading the pain in his lungs, and secondly through fear of his scattered enemies who could do something to revenge their loss. And so he wanted her both for the extreme care she took of him, and to protect her from any misfortune. He also loved her also for her great skills in providing good food for him.

The Emperor was happy to see his Empress, and he introduced his son Constantine to her and praised him before the Empress for his fighting skills.

Constantine was happy to meet his stepmother and greeted her courteously and respectfully.

The Caesar gave a toast for his son and enjoyed the revelries of that celebration which continued for several days.

***

But after a couple of weeks, the Caesar's health deteriorated and he was obliged to retire to bed again, for a few days, hoping to recover. But even so he could not rest for thinking about what he ought to do on the following days. As he was meditating on these things, Michael came to him. He was a Pict who had frequently deserted to the Emperor and then gone back to his own people. He had been forgiven by the Emperor and in consequence of this forbearance he now bore a deep affection towards him and for the rest of his life he planned and worked for the Emperor with all his heart and soul and always informed him of the plans of the Picts.

He came and said, "O Emperor, I have come to inform you that tomorrow the Picts will surround York and then commence another battle with the Romans. You should therefore anticipate them and draw up your lines outside the walls at daybreak."

"Thank you Michael. Not that my son is here I am more at peace. He has shown that he is a great and formidable general and I have nothing to fear. Go back to the Picts and tell them about my son Constantine. They are going to meet their death if they attack us. And moreover, a German army has recently arrived in York and will be ready to help me if attacked."

Michael did as he was told. He went away and spoke to the Picts' leader, "Do not be puffed up with pride, because your army is strong and numerous, and when you begin a battle with the Emperor's army do not raise your hopes too high because his numbers are small. For the Emperor's son might is invincible and a large mercenary army is already at his service. If you will not accept peace with him, the vultures will eat your corpses." This is what Michael said to the Picts.

Constantine asked his father why he would use a spy like Michael.

"Michael loves his country. He wants the best for his country. It is always right to cooperate with people like Michael because he wants peace, law and order, and prosperity for his country. That is what we want to bring here in Britain, and he understands that," said Constantius.

Constantine couldn't agree more. He also wanted his father to rest as his sickness was progressing rapidly. And Constantius listened to him. Constantine was the one leading the Romans.

Constantine was in constant communication with other generals who were more familiar with the terrain and the enemy. He listened to their suggestion about the capture of the numerous horses of the Picts which were grazing in the plain during night-time.

The plan worked out well. When spies detected the Picts' army, the intelligence was used right away. While the Picts were sleeping, the Roman soldiers entered into their camp and stole a great number of their horses.

The next day Constantine send the Picts a message to surrender.

When the leader of the Picts was informed early in the morning of Constantine's message and the fact that that his army had lost many of their horses, he pondered if he should fight or accept peace. It was a hard decision because his army was clearly at a disadvantage but he was a proud man and he decided that he still wanted war. And he planned a sudden attack.

As day dawned, all the Picts crossed the river and seemed eager to begin a battle.

Constantine at once mounted his horse, ordered the attack to be sounded, drew up his lines and himself took his stand before them. When he noticed that the Picts were coming to the attack recklessly, he ordered the skilled archers to keep their bows bent and shoot at his orders. He arranged his army in three wings and he himself held the centre of the army. He then ordered the archers to attack.

The archers made a bold attack on the Picts who, when the battle had just started, were trying to get closer to Constantine's cavalry. But the Picts seemed like easy prey without their horses. When Constantine ordered his cavalry to attack, the Picts became frightened either by the thick clouds of darts or by the sight of the shining armor of the Roman cavalry and Constantine's spirited fighting and they turned back, anxious to cross the river in their flight to their forests. The Romans pursued them at full speed, some hit them in the back with their arrows, while others hurled spears and javelins. Many indeed were slain even before they reached the edge of the river, still more, fleeing with all speed, fell into the torrent and were carried away and drowned. Constantine was clearly the champion of the day, and being proclaimed victor by his soldiers and generals, he returned back to York and gave the news of victory to the Emperor, his father Constantius.

***

Constantious was glad for this great victory but his health was taking a turn for the worst. Constantine and the other generals were by his side as much as they could.

As Constantious felt that his end was near, he made it very clear to his most trusted generals that he wanted his son Constantine to succeed him.

"Give me your word that you will make Constantine Emperor," he asked his generals.

The Generals had no objections. On the contrary, they had great respect for Constantine and wanted him to be their leader.

When Constantius died, Constantine felt sorry he lost the compassionate father he had just recently come to know.

It was July 25, 306.

As the body of Constantious lay dead in a coffin in the courthouse for people to pay their last homage to their Emperor, Constantine received consolations from many people, even locals.

The auxiliary unit known as the Regii, which had been formed by Constantius since 298 from a group of Alemans, who had been trapped on an island in the frozen river Rhine, stood by the coffin of the Emperor. Their King Crocus was there too, crying for the loss of the Emperor who had helped him in his hour of need. Constantius was buried with all honors of a great ceremony.

As soon as Constantius was laid to rest, all generals gathered in a meeting to discuss the situation. King Crocus was there too and he rose and proposed that Constantine should be declared Emperor right away because that was the will of the deceased Emperor.

So great was the generals" respect for Constantious that one after another they stood up and wanted to form an allegiance with Constantine. On that very day that Constantious was laid to rest, they wanted to see his son Constantine declared Emperor.

Constantine was invited in the meeting without knowing what was going on. He was wearing a soldier's uniform and he was asked to sit on the golden throne which was in a higher position, where his father used to sit. He was wearing sandals and he had a sword in his hand, the tip of which was resting on the ground.

One of the generals who had Constantius" crown in his hand approached Constantine on one side and Bishop Lactantius on the other. The general gave the crown to Lactantius.

Bishop Lactantius lifted the crown high in the air, and spoke out loudly.

"I have been told that all you generals want Constantine to become the new Emperor. Do you all agree that Constantine should get this crown?"

"Yes." said all the other generals and soldiers and they all lifted their swords high in the air.

Then he turned to Constantine.

"Do you accept this crown Constantine. Do you accept to be the leader of the West. Out of our free will, we choose to follow and obey you. Will you accept this crown."

Soldiers waited for Constantine's response.

Constantine, looking formidable, dressed rather as a soldier than an Emperor stood up, looking at the crowd.

The Bishop stood by his side with a golden wrath in his hands.

Constantine seemed touched by the kindness of the generals. Every one fell silent waiting for him to speak. Contantine looked up towards heaven and then towards the crowd and began to speak.

"Romans, Compatriots, Friends,

The Roman Empire does not need lip-service. It does not need lip service from its citizens, soldiers, generals, senate, not even from its Emperors. Rome needs real love, people who really care about her, people who love her and criticize her for her flaws, people who speak the truth, and above all, people who are willing to fight for her freedom and happiness and prosperity, till their last breath.

Rome does not need lip-service and then get stabbed in the back.

Rome needs a good leader and good citizens.

It's a great honor, that you think that I am qualified to be the Emperor of the West, your Emperor. It is indeed a difficult task to be a good Emperor. But I gladly accept such a difficult task, because as Pyrrhus put it, "How can I not be a great eagle, when I have such great wings to support me, when I am surrounded by such great eagles?"

There are not many promises I want to make today, but surely I will promise this. I will fight for Rome's freedom to the end. I will defend the Roman Empire for as long as I live. I will fight for the freedom and prosperity of all individuals and all groups. I will defend the individual rights of citizens and the rule of law.

I will protect the freedom of the Roman Empire with all my heart, mind, and soul, with all that I am and all that I have. I will not just sit in my palace and send my armies to fight. I will be at the head of the army myself, in the first line of fire, face to face with our enemies. I will do my best, use all my skills, to make the Roman Empire greater and ensure freedom for all. And for this reason, I gladly accept such a task."

Everyone in the palace hall stood up and long applauded the new Emperor.

"Long live the Emperor. Long live the great eagle of Illyria!" were the cheerful shouts of the crowd. When the applause died down, Lactantius spoke again.

"Then Constantine, you are officially our Caesar and Emperor," and he approached Constantine and placed the golden crown above his head. Constantine sat down in the throne, now as an Emperor. It was an impressive sight, for gold overlaid his throne and there was gold above his head. And yet Constantine was dressed as a soldier at barracks. He was a real barracks-Emperor, an Emperor of the people and soldiers.

Then Cracus, the Aleman king spoke.

"Never has a leader been more honored than chosen by the free will of the people," said the king. "In the name of all soldiers and generals gathered here today, I declare our allegiance to you, our Emperor, Your word is our command. Rule with justice, rule with great power, rule with a great heart."

"Long live our new Emperor" said the general.

"Long live our new Emperor" the crowd chanted again and gave Constantine a new round of applause.

"I think he could become the best Emperor we have ever had," said, Peter one of the guard soldiers at the door, talking to his friend, Vespian.

"That's how it seems at the moment. But only time will tell how good he is," Vespian said.

"He gave his word. We can trust his word. He is an Illyrian," replied Peter.

"Well, the fact that Constantine was chosen as Emperor without any fighting between the Generals and other possible candidates is surprising. From what we have seen so far, the Roman Empire is such that succession after the death of a ruler is often accompanied by a lot of trouble, and violent coups. But Constantine's rise to power has been an easy and natural and peaceful one. This much I will admit," said Vespian.

"Could this a sign that he has the backing of a strong God and of the people he rules then Vespian?" said Peter.

"It could be," said Vespian.

#

CHAPTER 5

THE RULE OF CONSTANTINE

COMING TO POWER as an Emperor was just the start of a great responsibility and Constantine knew that. Now he had to take care of his subjects and rule them and protect them from attacks. And attacks could come from any side, outside or inside of the Empire.

As soon, then, as he was established on the throne, Constantine began to care for the interests of his paternal inheritance and visited with much considerate kindness all those provinces which had previously been under his father's government.

He had to take care of the internal affairs of his Empire closely. He immediately directed his attention to the quarters of the world where he was Emperor, starting with the British nations. These accepted his rule and so Constantine proceeded to consider the state of the remaining portions of the Empire, that he might be ready to tender his aid wherever circumstances might require it.

Some tribes of the barbarians who dwelt on the banks of the Rhine, and the shores of the Western ocean, welcomed him right away. Others were a bit wary of the new Emperor and accepted him because they did not want to start a war.

As Constantine was continuing his visits in on the banks of the Rhine, some Franks tried to seize this opportunity and attacked Gaul.

Constantine immediately sent envoys to the Frank leader, to resolve the problem in a peaceful manner.

He was in Arles, in one of his palaces he had inherited from his father Constantius when the envoys sent to Robert, the Frank leader, returned and brought the latter's written message to the Emperor. Constantine read the letter immediately.

"It was certainly not against Your Majesty that I took the field, but simply in order to avenge the injustice done to my kinsman King Alan by your father Constantius. But if you desire peace with me, I too shall gladly welcome it, though only on condition that you are ready to fulfil the conditions signified to you by your ambassadors who visited me."

"His requests are absolutely impossible and injurious," said the main envoy. "The Frankish leader has requested a large amount of gold with which he can build a formidable army. Moreover, he has requested military assistance, whenever required. His conditions are such, as if a battle has been fought between you two and he is the victor and you are the loser," he added.

"So his real plan is clear then," Constantine said thoughtfully. "He has made requests as if he himself desired peace, but by making impossible ones and not obtaining them he would have recourse to arms, and thus attribute the blame for the war to Rome."

"Exactly," said the envoy.

"Well, there is no need to beat about the bush. Robert wants war and we will give it to him. Tell him exactly what he wants to hear. I do not accept his terms. He is in no condition to place terms. He will have peace only if there are no conditions put by him," said Constantine.

When the envoys sent the answer to Robert, he convoked all his commanders and addressed them.

"You all know the injustice done to my kinsman Alan by Constantius and the dishonor put upon my reign. Now that Constantius is dead, and his son Constantine has come to power, it's time to get our wealth and territory back. We know that now we have to deal with a new and young Emperor, who is a brave soldier and gifted with strategic knowledge far beyond his years, and with such a man we cannot go to war lightly. But to war we shall go because war is our only option at present. And we must go to war as always, to win. But in order to win, we have to give our best. Now wherever there is division of command, confusion results from the diversity of opinions. Hence it is necessary that all the rest of us should obey one single commander who must consult us all and not act on his own judgment heedlessly and casually; the rest of us should openly express our views, but at the same time be ready to follow the advice of the elected commander. And here I am, one of you all, ready to obey whomsoever you agree to elect as commander."

All approved of this proposition and declared that Robert had spoken well, and then unanimously awarded him the first place, because they feared him, not because they loved him.

But Robert simulated indifference and for some time refused the honor, trying to detect who among the commanders was ambitious to take his place. He wanted to get rid of all ambitious competitors. When three commanders expressed interest, he asked each of them to discuss things in private, and treacherously killed them one by one.

And finally he declared to all others that he had decided to be their leader, after further consideration.

Then he said to the commanders and key soldiers. "Listen to me, commanders and all the rest of you. We have left our own country in the hand of a Roman Emperor. We shall shortly have to fight against an Emperor who is very brave; although he has only recently assumed the reins of government, yet under the previous Emperors, as a soldier and general, he came out conqueror in many wars and brought back to them the fiercest rebels as captives of his sword, therefore we must enter upon this war with our whole heart and soul if we want to win. And if Mars, our patron god, should allot us the victory, we shall no longer be in need of money and land. Consequently we must enter into battle with him and win or die." To this all his army assented.

***

Constantine knew what he was supposed to do. He immediately prepared an army to meet the rebellious Franks in battle.

Fortunately for him, his late father had already created a good structure for emergency needs. Besides the Aleman auxiliary unit of Regii from the Rhine, there was the Frankish unit of Batavi, raised from among the Franks settled next to the Rhine. The Frankish Cornuti and Bracchiati, distinguished by their horned helmets and armbands, joined with him as well, as soon as he started his campaign toward Gaul.

With a big army, Constantine reached the Eastern side of Gaul.

The adversary francs were great soldiers and they were using a new weapon, a throwing axe they called francisca. It was indeed a very deadly weapon. The Cornuti and Bracchiati made this very clear to Constantine.

Constantine thanked them and asked their opinion on what best strategy to use against such adversaries. He did not want to get caught off-guard. He listened to them and followed their advice.

He ordered his soldiers to make franciscas too, so the enemy would not have an advantage. And besides this, Constantine was a great soldier and tactician. He knew that this first major battle was decisive because he needed to win the trust of the populace as well, not just that of the soldiers. He had to triumph.

The weather was out of joint that January. It was rainy at one moment, sunny at the next. And then it got really cold and it snowed. The temperature was icy when the armies met.

As the armies got closer to each other, the Franks thought that they had the upper hand. One could see the excitement before the battle on both sides as vapor rose from where both armies stood.

The infantry of both armies were in the front and cavalries were in the back. The Franks had never seen the Romans in this order before. They knew that the Romans thought that this was not a good way to arrange the army. Surprisingly they had chosen to do exactly that, the opposite of a normal line-up.

The Franks were getting closer and closer and eagerly waiting for their leader's order to throw their franciscas. Their leader was hesitating for some strange reason, even though they were now within throwing distance. And just when they thought that they would be the ones attacking first, a hail of franciscas from Constantine's infantry caught them completely off guard. Many were injured and disabled. Then Constantine's cavalry with the speed of light attacked from the sides. Both armies were now using their franciscas as their fighting weapons, not swords. Hitting a soldier with a francisca in his knew, arm, or back caused great damage. Often the solders would just throw a francisca over someone's head. The battle was brutal and bloody but in the end, the Frankish army was destroyed. Soon they were retreating in all directions.

Constantine captured the Frankish leader. As he was still very haughty and continued to throw insults at everyone, Constantine had him put in an iron cage.

In similar fashion he captured a few other rebel kings in the same area as well. And when the victory was complete, Constantine rode in triumph in Arles and paraded these royal captives in the streets and in the arena. As none of the barbarian leaders wanted peace or be part of the Roman Empire, they were thrown to the beasts.

The message to all rebellious barbarian leaders was clear. All those who attacked the Roman Empire would be punished severely.

These military successes were welcomed by people all over the Empire and Constantine was accepted as an Emperor not only by the troops but the majority of people in the Western Part of the Roman Empire, by the Gauls, Spaniards, Germans, and Picts.

#

CHAPTER 6

REBELLION OF MAXENTIOUS IN ROME

CONSTANTINE was enjoying his stay at his Palace in Arles and he spent his time enrolling recruits in the army and training them carefully in the art of stretching the bow, wielding the spear, throwing the francisca, riding on horseback, and making various formations. He also taught the soldiers the new system of marshalling the lines which he had invented himself; now and again he would ride with them and review the phalanxes and give seasonable suggestions. Spring had started when a messenger of Emperor of Italy Maximian came to his Palace.

"Emperor Maximian has been dethroned," the messenger said to Constantine.

"By whom?" asked Constantine, immediately concerned about the unexpected turn of these events.

"By his son, Maxentius," the messenger said. "Maximian is headed to Arles to seek your help," he added.

"What happened?" inquired Constantine making a sign to the messenger to sit down next to him.

"As you know, Maxentious, the son of Maximian, who lives in Rome and is married to Maximilla, the daughter of Emperor Galerius, is not a nice guy. Arrogantly, he has decided to declare himself Emperor of Italy. The fact that he is in Rome and related to both Maximian and Galerius makes him think that this is enough reason for him to claim the throne of Italy," the messenger said.

"And what did Maximian do? He could not accept this so easily, could he?" Constantine asked.

"Maximian was against it of course. He tried to reason with his son Maxentius to give up his plans and wait for his time to take the reigns of his Empire. But Maxentius could not wait. And as he got control of the praetorians of Rome, he quarreled with his father Maximian. Maximian asked him to pay obeisance, or face his wrath. Maxentius refused the adoratio to him very publicly. That was just the start. The next day Maxentius invited the Emperor to a dinner through a "reconciling" message which said this. "Father, I have crossed a red line and I would like to apologize. Come over and let's discuss the question of the throne in private at the dinner table. My family and I would be happy if you come to dine with us. We have prepared a good meal, not wanting in variety and good flavor and best fruits of the season. We want you to share this banquet with us. Looking forward to meeting you and settling all our disputes." That same day, just before Maximian was leaving for the banquet, a spy told him that Maxentius was planning to kill him. Maximian could not believe his ears. Distressed he grasped his beard for a time pondering what to do next. He immediately went back to his Palace, and together with his entire family and many guards, decided to flee Rome. After he left, Maxentius forced the Roman senate to declare Maximian as dethroned and him as the new Emperor. That's why Maximian is coming here, to ask for your help and protection," the messenger said.

"The situation is not at all clear in Rome. I can't believe it that Maxentious, the only son of Maximian, is doing this to his father, the legitimate Emperor of Italy. I can't believe he has usurped the throne of his father in Rome," Constantine said shaking his head.

"Maxentius is a beast, not an Emperor. I can assure you, he will soon claim the West and even the entire Roman Empire. Because Maxentius had control of the praetorians, Maximian had no choice but to leave, together with his wife and his daughter Fausta," the messenger said.

"Are they far away?" Constantine asked.

"They are staying in a small town close to Arles. Maximian has nobody else to turn to at this moment but you Constantine. Are you going to help him," the messenger said concerned that Constantine was not going to be of assistance to him.

"Of course I will. I will be his friend in need. I stand for the rule of law," Constantine said proudly and these words calmed the messenger.

The messenger went back to inform Maximian about Constantine's decision. It was not long before Maximian arrived at the Palace of Constantine in Arles.

When he arrived, the Emperor of Italy told Constantine how humiliated he felt that his son had usurped his throne. He humbly asked Constantine for his protection and cooperation.

Constantine welcomed him as the true legal Emperor of Italy, with all honors and pomp. He promised to put his armies at his disposal to regain his throne.

***

As soon as Emperor Maximian left, Maxentious started to act as the Emperor of Italy.

The same year he captured power, there was a draught in his country. The economy was going to tatters. There were shortages of everything. But Maxentius was a ruthless leader. He started taxing Romans, something that had never been done before. He also stopped bringing supplies of food for the populace from Egypt, the bread basket of the Roman Empire. Food was provided only for his soldiers. Not only did Maxentious treat his subjects ruthlessly but he also could not refrain from all vice and evil deeds. He was seducing senators" daughters. All these weakened his power and he soon began to be viewed as a tyrant by people in Italy.

As a senior Emperor, Galerious thought that it was his duty to make Maxentious to give up his claim. He crossed the Adriatic with a big army and sent a letter to Maxentius, ordering him to give up his claim as Emperor of Rome. But Maxentious did not want to listen to him. So Galerius together with Severus, the Emperor of Illyricum, invaded Italy and tried to depose Maxentious, but in vain. Maxentious was victorious and Severus was killed and Galerius was forced to leave Italy in a hurry with the remaining troops.

***

Unhappy about these developments, Galerius summoned the Emperors, Constantine, the dethroned Maximian, and Max Daia who replaced Severus, and some other main leaders to a conference in Carnuntum on November 18, 308. Galerius sent a message to Maxentious again to resign or face the force of all the Roman troops. But Maxentious refused again.

Galerius also tried to revive the system of two Augusti only ruling the Empire but his efforts were not successful. The system of tetrarchy prevailed again.

Constantine had rulership of the west including Gaul, Spain, and Britain. Maximian was supposed to be the Emperor of Italy. Max Daia was the ruler of Illyricum and Galerius of the East.

As Galerius died in 311, Licinius replaced him. But Maxentious decided to claim the entire Roman Empire for himself. Constantine clearly refused and told Maxentious to stay away from the Western Empire and give up his plans to get Constantine's part.

But Maxentius was not discouraged.

It was at this time that Maximian asked Constantine to marry his daughter Fausta, in order to seal their friendship. Constantine agreed to get married to Fausta.

When Constantine and Fausta got married, Maximian gave the throne of Italy to Constantine.

"If you can get the throne of Rome from Maxentius, it is yours, I don't want it. By you having it is the same as me having it," Maximian told him.

Constantine was impressed by Maximian's generosity and accepted the gift graciously.

***

As Maxentius continued to claim the West, Constantine felt impelled to act against Maxentious first. It was not wise to stay on the defense. He had to move into the offense.

So in 312, Constantine struck across the Alps into Italy. In Mediolanum, he made a deal with Licinius, Emperor of the east, to support each other and if victorious, to divide the Roman Empire in two parts.

To consolidate power and to seal their alliance, Licinius got engaged to Constantine's half-sister, Constantia.

While Licinius was sent to defend territories in the north, Constantine rode towards Rome.

At the same time, Maxentious made a deal with Max Daia.

Constantine entered into Italy unopposed. The misinformed army sent against him by Maxentious missed them completely and that put Constantine into great advantage. After getting this bad news, Maxentious decided to wait for Constantine in Rome and kept many of his soldiers there.

Constantine had about 90 thousand infantry and 8000 cavalry.

The first city that Constantine seized was segusio. As it was the custom, soldiers wanted to plunder the town but Constantine did not allow them.

"We are here on a War of Liberation, not of conquest," he told his soldiers. He talked to the leaders of Segusio and they accepted his rule. He let them rule as before. And with this act, he won the heart of the Italians. And news of this great deed spread throughout Italy.

Everybody there was now saying that Constantine had come to liberate Italy from the tyrant and illegitimate Emperor, Maxentious. And people did not like Maxentious. Nobody. They thought of him as a tyrant who needs to be removed as quickly as possible. They hated him. They were ready to fight against him and remove him from his usurped power.

The next serious fighting was in Augusta Taurinarum (Turin). Constantine's strategy was impeccable once again. His center gave way before the clibannarii, who then found themselves assailed and encircled by Constantine's soldiers with iron-bound clubs. The clibannarrii fought hard and managed to make an opening and retreated towards their town, with Constantine's troops on their heels. But as soon as they approached the castle, the citizens closed the gates to them and Constantine won an easy victory. The citizens were all on Constantine's side.

Clearly the town was not looted, and this paid useful dividends. This made victory easier in Verona, Aquileia, Mutina (Modena). By the middle of October 312, the road to Rome lay open to Constantine's army.

When Maxentius learned of the fall of so many cities in Italy he became depressed. As he surrounded himself with flatterers, they all heartened him with false hopes and assured him that those cities could be recovered easily.

"The only needful thing is that your Majesty should be safe. And as for the captors of the cities, they shall render fourfold that which they have taken," his close advisors told him.

Then indeed, Maxentius became happy again and spent the rest of the days free from care. The advisors had to do this because they were aware of Maxentius' extreme stupidity. They naturally did not want to fall from his good favor and become his prey because Maxentius was ruthless and merciless to all those he did not like.

#

CHAPTER 7

THE BATTLE OF THE MILVIAN BRIDGE

"AN ENEMY OF ROME will die in this war". The words of the pagan priest rang in Maxentius ears as he was preparing to meet with his generals. They would be happy about the sybelline prophecy given to him about the battle with Constantine. He could not wait to share this news with them at his Palace. His decision to meet with the sybelline priests had paid off.

As he had been waiting anxiously in Rome, he had not resisted the temptation to know the result of the battle before it happened. Constantine's army had been getting closer by the hour and he had been victorious in many cities of Italy. The situation was tense. Maxentius was ready to do anything to win this battle. Anything. That's why Maxentius had decided to consult the pagan priests in the first place. He had faith in sybelline prophecies. He had asked the priests about the outcome of the next battle he was going to fight, against Constantine. He couldn't have been happier when the high priest told him "An enemy of Rome will die in this war."

Finally the generals made it to his palace. Maxentius had a big grin in his face when he told them the good news.

"The pagan priests have never been wrong in their prediction. I asked them about the battle with Constantine. You know what they told me. They told me that an enemy of Rome will die in this war," Maxentius said.

"You are the Emperor of Rome since you dethroned your father Maximian. You are now Rome. And Constantine is your enemy. This is indeed good news," said one of the generals.

All Maxentius" generals nodded their heads.

"Tell us what to do," said one of the generals.

"This is my advice to you. Engage Constantine's army as soon as you see it and fight a big battle. The fighting will be too heavy for them after their long trip and numerous battles. I will be there too, watching as this unfolds. We are going to give them hell. We will hit them first and hit them hard. They are weak and we are strong. Many of them are wounded and we are all in good health. Victory is ours," Maxentius said to his generals in a cocksure voice.

The generals agreed.

"We will give them hell," said one the bloodthirsty generals.

Maxentius ordered his spies to go out and find out the whereabouts of the Constantine's army and report back as soon as they did.

As Constantine's army was very close to the city of Rome, it was not hard for the spies to find the army and come back with intelligence to Maxentius.

"An army of about 100,000 was approaching River Tiber!" a spy told him.

"That is a big army but ours will be bigger. Tell my generals to have an army of 200,000 ready," said Maxentius.

***

Constantine was very tired of the long trip he and his army had done. He and his army desperately needed some rest. They were getting closer to Rome and the decisive big battle could happen at any time. It was the midday of October 28, 312.

At the hour when the sky sheds its light most generously, Constantine got off his white horse with a jump, let it loose to graze on the green grass, while he himself fell to his knees praying for a sign from God. He knew that a victory against Maxentius was very difficult. His army outnumbered his. The praetorians that fought on Maxentius' side were just as combat-hardened and courageous as those on his side. They were mostly from the same region and stock of people, Illyrians. Only divine help could tip the balance in his favor.

As he was on his knees praying with his hands joined together and his head up towards the sky, it seemed to him that God tore apart a veil in the sky that prevents humans from seeing God's supernatural signs. He turned his head towards the sun.

The sunrays had never been so warm and gentle and soothing and for the first time, they were not hurting or blinding his eyes. There in the sky Constantine saw a cross of light. And suddenly he heard a whisper in his ear: "In this sign there is victory." In a moment everything disappeared. Constantine remained speechless. He wondered what all this meant. He desperately needed divine assistance. The sign of the cross of light could be the sign from God.

He spent the day in deep thoughts. When the night came and he fell asleep, he had a dream that reaffirmed his earlier vision. God told him that the sign he had received was from him and it would make him invincible in all his battles. When Constantine woke up, he knew he had to talk to Bishop Lactantius.

When in the morning Lactantius heard the story, he told Constantine that in his view, God himself had talked to him. Constantine did not hesitate any longer. He immediately converted to Christianity. Led by the Bishop, he fell down on his knees, thanked God for the sign and accepted Jesus as his Lord and Savior.

Constantine felt very alive after that vision and his conversion. Many thoughts were racing in his mind. His senses all came alive in an extraordinary way. His whole being felt full of energy and strength. His mind also was working faster and better.

***

He had to arrange his army the way he wanted. The right man at the right spot.

He thought of each of his generals and strong men, their skills and shortcomings.

Each key man had to deal with a different situation. But overall, the skills of each man had to serve a general purpose. Victory. So each of the skills had to be combined. And all the shortcomings had to be covered. And that is where team work came into play. Without it, victory would be impossible.

If they had that faith and confidence that working together achieves better results victory would be easier. Constantine knew he had to instill that kind of cooperation among his troops, in order to make them invincible. It was true, a strong man could do much at times, but if he did not have a good team to support him, he would sooner or later be dead. The field of the battle spared no-one. Chances for survival and success increased only as cooperation and team efforts increased. And he himself had to be the leader of the team, not just a strong general.

Constantine stood up and whistled to his horse which immediately came close to him. He mounted the horse and then he moved in front of his army and gave the order to all his soldiers to put the sign of the cross and letters Chi Ra on their shields.

The soldiers were at first surprised at this unusual order, but they did as their General ordered them. Soon they started inquiring about this and Constantine told them everything. He told them about his vision. He told them how they were going to fight. He told them how they were going to win.

"Good soldiers follow orders. Follow my orders. Fight with courage but fight with caution as well. Don't do crazy stupid things. A dead soldier is no good. So stay alive. Fight wisely. Use your head and your heart," Constantine told them.

The passion in Constantine's voice raised the soldiers" morale.

Many believed that the sign was true and thus united in their faith they continued their march towards Rome.

They had to stop for the night in some forest nearby and continue their journey early in the morning after a good breakfast.

The army of Maxentious was moving in the opposite direction that morning. They soon noticed Constantine's army far beyond the Milvian Bridge that spanned River Tiber. They moved fast to cross the bridge.

As Constantine's army was slowly moving towards Maxentious" army, Constantine raised his hand and ordered his troops to stop. He got off his horse and fell on his knees, bowed his head and raised his hands towards heaven.

His soldiers followed suit and all fell on their knees even though he didn't ask them to.

Constantine prayed to the Christian God. His words just came to him as if from above.

Supreme God, I beseech you; holy God, I beseech you. I commend all justice to you, I commend our safety to you. Through you we live, through you we can emerge victorious and fortunate. Supreme, holy God, hear my prayers, I stretch my arms to you; listen, holy, supreme God. In the name of your Son, Jesus Christ.

When he saw Constantine's army on their knees, Maxentius started mocking Constantine in the presence of his generals. "They"re already on their knees! I don't even see the point of fighting against them! And their numbers are half ours, just as I was told." He was now double sure that he would be victorious.

As soon as all his army crossed the Milvian Bridge, he had it destroyed so that no soldier of his would have a way to run back. The bridge was set on fire.

Maxentius knew that a cornered army would fight harder. He did not even have to say anything to tell them that only victory would save them. His army was now between the River Tiber and Constantine's army. He was sure that his soldiers got the message, "victory or death". And he was sure that it was going to be victory. The oracles had assured him of this.

After prayer, Constantine and his army stood up. Horsemen got on their horses. Infantry started to rattle their shields. The excitement before the battle was great. They were ready to meet the enemy face to face.

Both Emperors took their time to organize and arrange their armies. Maxentious stayed to the left side of his army, to a corner where the river turned, seemingly the most defended spot, but with no way to escape if challenged and overcome.

Constantine knew immediately what to do. He had to pretend that his army would focus his efforts on the opposite side from where Maxentius was standing on his horse, trying to break their line there, and with then with the flower of his army in the heat of battle, with the speed of light, boldly attack Maxentious on the other side, break the line of his praetorians and attack Maxentius himself. He shared his plan with his closest friends who agreed unanimously.

A fearful and deadly battle started on the right side. Soon many soldiers on both sides threw themselves at each other. Those who couldn't resist, started to lose their heads, their arms, their legs.

"Constantine is a brave man but his army will be annihilated very quickly" Maxentious said to his right wing general, who was standing by him. "He chose to attack the strongest part of my army. Even if God were behind Constantine's charge, his failure is unavoidable. He couldn't have made a worse decision. To seal this victory I will send half of my praetorians over there too."

The general nodded and said, "I agree Emperor."

Half of Maxentius praetorians rode to the spot where the fighting was the fiercest. But as the battle was raging on the right side, Constantine and many of his Praetorian guards and all his horsemen, abandoned the battle there and quickly galloped towards Maxentious.

Taken by surprise, Maxentious and his soldiers and officers and generals saw them riding like the wind but they had no time to respond to it and stop them at a safe distance. Most of his horsemen were already engaged in the battle. Only a few of them were available.

Constantine and his strong contingent of Praetorians on horseback attacked Maxentius and his forces with great fury. It was as if an eagle had landed among some pigeons, decapitating them. Constantine's soldiers threw many an adversary from their horses and soon found themselves very close to Maxentious and his Praetorians. A terrible and tough horse-battle began to rage in that quarter.

The river was turbulent and full of whirlpools. Soon dead bodies were scattered in the water and along the riverbank. Now Maxentious regretted his decision to destroy the bridge. He had no route of escape for himself. His only escape would be to swim across the river. He looked at the river. The sharp shining swords of his enemies seemed more menacing and he decided to try what seemed most logical under those circumstances.

He got off his black horse and jumped into the cold water of the river. He wanted to take his heavy armor off but then he knew that the arrows would pierce him. So he decided to keep it on thinking he was strong enough to swim with it on. He managed to make it to the middle of the river. He was struggling and he was hoping he would be able to make it to the other side. But the steely armor was feeling heavier and heavier and the water colder and colder. And suddenly, all his strength left him and after waiving his hands for a few more moments, he went down in the water and drowned.

His soldiers saw him disappear in the river and their courage seeped out of them. Some of them tried to do exactly what their general had done before them, try to cross the river. They jumped into water without thinking if they could cross the river or not. One of them as he was jumping his clothes remained caught on a broken tree branch and just at that moment an arrow pierced his side. Most of the others who managed to get into water had the same fate as Maxentious. They drowned because of their heavy armor and because the water of the river was very cold or because they were hit by arrows or spears. Only a lucky few managed to get on the other side and survive. They ran away as fast as they could towards Rome.

Constantine's army was pushing their adversaries closer and closer to the river. As some horses bumped against some boats and tree trunks and big stones along the river, many horsemen were thrown off their saddles and fell into the cold water. They survived but they were not able to fight anymore. They knew that they were now easy prey and they decided to surrender.

Their surrender discouraged many others who followed their suit. Only a few decided to fight to the end, to die not to win. And that's exactly what happened. They were too few to change the result of the battle.

Soon the bugler sounded the sound of victory for Constantine. All his soldiers rejoiced and shouted "Victory! Victory! Long Live Constantine! Long Live Constantine!"

A group of soldiers took a boat and started searching for Maxentious's body. Soon they found it at the end of the river and decapitated it.

"An enemy of Rome died today!" said one of the soldiers.

They put his head in a spear and thus Constantine and his soldiers rode to Rome. The citizens opened the gates of their city and welcomed him as a liberator. Constantine's good reputation had preceded him.

"Liberty! Liberty!" was the shout of the exuberant crowd.

#

CHAPTER 8

CONSTANTINE AND LICINIUS SHARE POWER

"AND SO CONSTANTINE entered Rome on October 29, 312?" Licinius asked Julius, the Roman envoy that he had sent to Rome, to find out what was going on in the Western Part of the Roman Empire.

"Yes. He staged a grand adventus in the city, and was met with popular jubilation. Maxentius' body was fished out of the Tiber and decapitated. His head was paraded through the streets of Rome for all to see. Maxentius became the laughing stock of Romans," Julius said, while he had a look at the luxurious palace of Licinius, with all the servants around him.

"So it was a complete victory, welcomed by everybody in Rome," Licinius said.

"Not only by people in Rome. After the ceremonies there, Maxentius' head was sent to Carthage so it would offer no further resistance. And the ploy was successful. Carthage opened the gates to Contantine's army as well," Julius said.

"Is Constantine in Rome at present? What is he doing?" Licinius asked

"Yes he is in Rome. Being a man of unvarying energy, he undertook the whole management of the affairs, and began directing everything himself. He took possession of the palace at sunrise and before even shaking off the dust of combat or allowing his body any rest, he was wholly plunged in thought about economic, political and other matters. His Bishop Lactantius, whom he reverences as a father, he made his confidant on all matters, as he did his mother Helen, and they both assist him in the administration of the Empire. Constantine first directed his attention to the most urgent question, taxes, which Maxentius had put on the people of Rome. He removed them again. And then he considered military matters, creating a rapid deployment force to protect the Empire from any sudden attacks of the barbarians," Julius said.

"Did he offer the customary sacrifices at the Temple of Jupiter?" asked Licinius who wanted to know every detail.

"Unlike his predecessors, Constantine neglected to make the trip to the Capitoline Hill and perform customary sacrifices at the Temple of Jupiter. I take this to mean that he does not believe in Jupiter as god. He has another God," Julius said.

"Hm! He seems to be quite serious about his Christian religion and God, if he ignored going to the Capitoline Hill," Licinius said.

"He did, however, choose to honor the Senatorial Curia with a visit, where he promised to restore its ancestral privileges and give it a secure role in his reformed government. He promised there would be no revenge against Maxentius" supporters," Julius said.

"That is not a good idea. He should have killed them. They may revolt again in the future," said Licinius.

"He decided to be merciful. All applauded his action. The Senate honored him too. It decreed him "the title of the first name", which means that his name will be listed first in all official documents, and acclaimed him as "the greatest Augustus"," Julius said.

"I"m already jealous. Why don't I have the same honors. I want to be "the greatest Augustus"," said Licinius.

"Constantine issued decrees returning property lost under Maxentius, inviting political exiles to return to Rome, and releasing all Maxentius" imprisoned opponents," Julius said.

"And I am assuming that Constantine is systematically purging Maxentius" image from all public places as well," Licinius said.

"That's correct. Maxentius has been written up as an evil tyrant. The current senate is also trying to remove Maxentius" influence on Rome's urban landscape. All structures built by Maxentius are being re-dedicated to Constantine, including the Temple of Romulus and the Basilica of Maxentius. At the focal point of the basilica, a stone statue of Constantine holding the Christian labarum in its hand has been erected. Its inscription bears the message that the statue has already made clear: By this sign Constantine freed Rome from the yoke of the tyrant, Maxentius," Julius said.

"So Constantine is overwriting all Maxentius" achievements," Licinius said.

"Where he has not overwritten Maxentius" achievements, Constantine is upstaging them: the Circus Maximus is being redeveloped so that its total seating capacity is twenty-five times larger than that of Maxentius" racing complex on the Via Appia. Maxentius" strongest supporters in the military have been neutralized. His Praetorian Guard and Imperial Horse Guard have been disbanded. On November 9, 312, barely two weeks after Constantine captured the city, the former base of the Imperial Horse Guard was chosen for redevelopment into the Lateran Basilica. The Legio II Parthica was removed from Alba and the remainder of Maxentius" armies were sent to do frontier duty on the Rhine, like a Rapid Deployment Force," Julius said.

"Thank you Julius for this detailed information. I need to be careful in my relations with Constantine. He is taking too much power and I need to have just as much or more," Licinius said.

"That is not all," Julius said.

Licinius raised his eyebrows.

"What else do you have Julius?" Licinius asked.

"He has invited you to Milan to secure your allegiance by your marriage to his half-sister Constantia," Julius said.

"I have already agreed to this arranged marriage. So it's too late to change anything. It is certain now that Constantine wants to gradually consolidate his military superiority over the Roman Empire. I have to remain friends with him until my throne is secure," Licinius said.

***

Lactantius was happy that Eusebius of Caesarea, a fellow bishop and a brother in Christ, came to visit him in his small church in Rome. They shared similar views on the Bible and the Christian God. Lactantius told Eusebius that he was a close friend of Constantine and things were going in the right direction for Christians.

"The victory in the big battle at the Milvian Bridge has changed Constantine radically. He put the Christian God to test and God proved to Constantine that He was more powerful than the pagan gods," Lactantius said.

"Is this a strong conviction of Constantine or just a fleeting opinion?" asked Eusebius.

"Definitely a conviction of the strongest kind. The sign of the cross of light he was given by God and the battle he won, has changed his worldview completely. He was sure even during the battle that he needed some more powerful aid than his military forces could afford him. And so he sought Divine assistance, deeming the possession of arms and a numerous soldiery of secondary importance, but believing the cooperating power of Deity invincible and not to be shaken," Lactantius said.

"How can you be so sure Lactantius?"

"He considered before the battle, on what God he might rely for protection and assistance. While engaged in this inquiry, he had the vision of Christ who gave him a sign of the cross of light and the words "In this sign there is victory." He believes that the sign of the cross is God's signature. After the vision, it occurred to him that, of the many Emperors who had preceded him, those who had rested their hopes in a multitude of gods, and served them with sacrifices and offerings, had in the first place been deceived by flattering predictions, and oracles which promised them all prosperity, but they had been disappointed and at last had met with an unhappy end. Not one of their gods had stood by, to warn them of the impending wrath of heaven," Lactanius said.

"So Constantine pursued an entirely opposite course," said Eusebius.

"Yes. He condemned their error and honored the one Supreme God. And he was rewarded for his faithfulness. He found the true God to be the Savior and Protector of the Roman Empire, and the Giver of every good thing. He reflected on this, well weighing the fact that they who had trusted in many gods had fallen by manifold forms of death, without leaving behind them either family or offspring, stock, name, or memorial among men. He trusted the Christian God completely, with all his heart and mind. The Christian God had given him manifestations of his power and very many tokens in the past. But the greatest sign was his victory in the Battle at the Milvian Bridge.

Constantine has no doubts as to who gave him that victory against Maxentius the tyrant. The tyrant's soldiers who had marched to the battle-field under the protection of a multitude of gods, had met with a dishonorable end. Many of Maxentius" soldiers had shamefully retreated from the battle without a blow. Many others had being slain in the midst of his own troops, and became, as it were, the mere sport of death. I am sure that Constantine knows that it is folly indeed to join in the idle worship of those who are no gods. He honors only the true God, the Christian God," Lactantius said.

"So you think that a great measure of gratitude has filled Constantine's heart," said Eusebius.

"Yes, that is true. Constantine's mind is only searching for ways how to show this gratitude to the God who gave such a precious victory to him. And just look at his banner now, the Standard of the Cross, which the Romans now call the Labarum, a long spear, overlaid with gold, forming the figure of the cross by means of a transverse bar laid over it. On the top of the whole is fixed a wreath of gold and precious stones, and within this, the symbol of the Savior's name, two letters indicating the name of Christ by means of its initial characters, the letter P being intersected by X in its center. These same letters, the Emperor is in the habit of wearing on his helmet. From the crossbar of the spear is suspended a cloth, a royal piece, covered with a profuse embroidery of most brilliant precious stones which, being also richly interlaced with gold, present an indescribable degree of beauty to the beholder. This banner is of a square form.

The Emperor has decided to use this sign as a safeguard against every adverse and hostile power and commanded that others similar to it should be carried at the head of all his armies, and displayed on top of public buildings" Lactantius said.

"That is impressive indeed. One more question Lactantius. Does Constantine still pray to the Christian God?" asked Eusebius.

"Most fervently. Constantine is so grateful for what the Christian God has done for him, for redeeming his soul and for the historic victory at the Milvian Bridge. I am sure that Constantine will be God's faithful servant now and forever," Lactantius said.

"I would like to meet him," said Eusebius.

"He will be happy to receive you," said Lactantius.

***

Constantine and Lactantius arrived at Constantine's Palace on two white horses. The servants sent them to Constantine immediately.

Constantine shook hands with both of them and asked them to feel at home and sit on his sofas. After exchanging courtesies, Lactantius began talking about the dire situation of some Christians.

"As you know Constantine many Christians are not free yet," Lactantius said.

"What can I do to remedy the situation Lactantius?" Constantine asked.

"You love what is right and hate what is wrong. Therefore, God, has blessed you, giving you more victory than anyone else on earth. You promised freedom for all. Defend Christians from persecution. Revoke Diocletian's and Galerius" decree for the persecution of Christians in the entire Roman Empire," Lactantius said.

"I agree. I have to talk to Licinius about this too," said Constantine.

Constantine did not forget Lactantius request. In fact, he could not get his words out of his head. He wanted to do something to show his gratitude to his Christian God and Lactantius" suggestion seemed the best thing he could think of.

He had invited Licenius to Milan and they were going to meet in February 313. That was the time when he could discuss the situation with him and do something for the Christian community. Constantine was quite sure that Licinius would not pose any problems in this regard and accept this proposal. Two years earlier, Licinius had agreed to engage Constantine's younger half-sister, Constantia, and that was an extra guarantee that he would continue to cooperate.

Licinius did arrive in Rome in February. He was to marry Constantia and become Constantine's brother-in-law. Constantine saw him as a trustworthy co-Emperor.

Things went as predicted. The wedding of Licinius and Constantia took place in the Royal Palace. It was a great event. It seemed that this sealed their friendship and rule.

This meant the start of a new allegiance. They agreed they were going to divide the Roman Empire in two parts.   Constantine would have control of the west and Licinius of the east. Constantine talked to Licinius about the Christians as well.

"Now that we are Emperors we need to produce decrees worthy of Imperial Majesty, concerning public good and security and safety and freedom for all. We will treat all our citizens as equal. Christians have been persecuted a lot in recent years. We got to change that. Religious tolerance should replace the old policy. Don't you agree?"

"There is no need for haste," said Licinius, as he did not have a very high regard for the Christians.

"No, but this is a pressing matter. Persecution has to be stopped immediately. And we can change this right away," Constantine said.

Licinius paused for a moment. Noticing Constantine's insistence, Licinius decided to keep his opinion to himself.

"If you think it's so important, I think we should go ahead then," Licinius said finally. "But I am not a Christian and don't expect me to be. I will just support your policy," he added.

"You don't have to be a Christian. You are free to make your own choice Licinius! That is exactly the point I was making! But as Emperors, we should allow Christians to make their free choice as well. Let them be and let them worship freely their God."

"So you want me to sign such an agreement"

"I insist," said Constantine. "You are the ruler of the Eastern Empire and we want peace in that part as well. You know that Maximinus Daia, who currently controls Illyria, resisted Galerius" dying wish after he had been plagued by sickness, that the persecution of Christians be ended. Daia is still persecuting Christians. He was in alliance with Maxentius and he is our enemy now, especially yours. I am pretty sure that he will attack you soon, because he will not accept your rule in the East. Moreover, people need to see that you are different from him. Otherwise, why would they support you instead of him. This will make our job easier of establishing your rule and unseating him because you will have more support."

Licencius thought about what Constantine told him for a moment. Constantine was right on this. This was a good way to gain the support of people, including Christians, in the East and defeat Maximinus Daia. This was on his favor.

"I see your point. I am ready to sign the decree," said Licenius.

The servants brought the written document in the room where both Emperors were. It was already written and just needed their signature. The document had special benefits for Christians, legalizing their religion and granting them restoration for all property seized during Diocletian's persecution and their freedom to worship their God freely. It was a document which declared universal religious toleration. Both Emperors signed the document. It was the end of February 313 and in March the document was spread across the Roman Empire and made public to all.

"When I, Constantine Augustus, and I, Licinius Augustus, happily met at Milan and had under consideration all matters which concerned the public good and security, we thought that among all the other things that would profit men generally that which merited our first and chief attention was reverence for the divinity. Our purpose is to grant both to the Christians and to all others the freedom to follow whichever religion they might wish; whereby whatsoever divinity dwells in heaven may be appeased and made propitious towards all who have been set under our power."

All Christians loved the Edict of Milan. Freedom to all seemed a fair idea to them. They liked it because it repudiated past methods of religious coercion. Some Christians were surprised that even Licinius had signed it.

As soon as the document became public, news reached the Emperors that Max Daia had declared war on Licinius. Licinius departed immediately with a great army. A great number of Christians in the eastern part of the Roman Empire decided to support Licinius in his military campaign to defeat Max Daia.

***

Defeating Maximinus Daia was decisive for Licinius. He wanted to be the sole ruler in the East. Licinius had left a garrison in Byzantium, which Maximinus attempted to win over with bribes.

They were Christians and refused. When this failed he tried to displace them by force. The garrison resisted for eleven days long enough to send word to Licinius, who hurried east.

Max Daia who was in Nicomedia decided to sail across the Bosphorus into Europe, meeting resistance from another of Licinius' garrisons at Heraclia in Thrace. Daia's army of 30 thousand continued its march and reached a staging post eighteen miles beyond Adrianople.

Licinius'' army headed in that direction to meet with Daia's army. As the armies approached each other, it seemed that a battle would shortly take place. Daia then made a vow to Jupiter that, if he won the victory, he would obliterate and utterly destroy the Christian name.

Licinius, in turn, on the eve of battle with Daia, told Christians to pray for the fate of the battle. Christians prayed the same prayer that Constantine prayed before the Battle at the Milvian Bridge: "Supreme God, we beseech you; holy God, we beseech you. We commend all justice to you, we commend our safety to you, we commend our Empire to you. Through you we live, through you we emerge victorious and fortunate. Supreme, holy God, hear our prayers, we stretch our arms to you; listen, holy, supreme God."

The prayer appealed to all soldiers and the troops intoned it three times on their knees on the field of battle, before engaging and defeating Maximinus'' forces on April 30, 313.

Licenius made for Nicomedia. To win the support of Christians, he repealed Daia's persecution and on June 13, he erected for all to see an inscribed version of the letter he and Constantine had formulated in Milan. He instructed that copies of the letter be dispatched to all cities and towns in the eastern realm and that they be displayed prominently attached to rulings by local magistrates, so that the will of the Emperors would no longer be suppressed.

Daia, who had fled the battlefield, was pursued to Tarsus, where he tried to commit suicide.

The poison Daia ingested failed because he was so engorged with food and wine, leaving the man deranged for four days; in that time, he pounded his head so hard against a rock that his eyes popped out.

Branded as a tyrant, statues of Daia now were cast down throughout the Empire. His wife, his eight-year-old son and his seven year-old daughter were all put to death in Antioch. So were other potential rivals: Valeria, daughter of Diocletian and Galerius'' widow, was murdered; her mother Prisca and her adopted son, Candidianus, met the same fate. Candidianus had been betrothed to Daia's young daughter. Severianus, son of the former Augustus Severus, was executed.

Now, only two imperial families remained, that of Licinius and that of Constantine, united through Constantia who, in 315, gave birth to a son. Valerius Licinianus Licinius.

Licinius' hopes and claims for his son immediately became an issue between the Emperors. He was jealous about the future of Constantine's son, Crispus.

\#

CHAPTER 9

THE WARS OF THE AUGUSTI

BECAUSE CONSTANTINE did not have any kids with Fausta, he moved to ensure the succession of Crispus, his only son by Minervina, right after Licinius became a father in 315. Still too young to properly play a role in administering the Empire, Crispus was to become a Ceasar alongside a second man, Bassianus, a Roman senator who was certainly old enough to govern, and was married to one of the three half-sisters of Constantine, Anastasia, after Licinius had married Constantia.

The wedding of Bassianus and Anastasia, took place during Constantine's sojourn in Rome, from July to the end of September 315. Bassianus was, therefore, brother-in-law to both Augusti, because of Constantine and Constantia, and was to be entrusted with Italy, including Rome.

The status of Italy, and more particularly of Rome, had been a bone of contention between the Augusti for some time. Now that Licinius' power in the East was established and an heir was born to him, he wanted to change what had happened in the past, and make sure that his son would rule in the future. He thought of the course of events and he found good reasons to fight against Constantine. Constantine's acquisition of Rome in 312, and with it, the whole of Italy, had violated Licinius" interests.

Dwelling in the past, and not understanding the new situation that had been created in the Empire, Licinius became jealous of Constantine's success. The grass seemed greener on the other side.

Neither of the Augusti actually resided in Rome.

Constantine shuttled between Arles and Trier in Gaul, while Licinius established his court at Sirmium in Pannonia.

Rome was part of the west and Licinius coveted Rome. When in July 315, the senate decided to celebrate Constantine's victory and dicennalia together, in stone, by dedicating a triumphal arch to him in Rome, and offering prayers of thanks for his continued rule, this was a monumental poke in Licinius" eye and the straw that broke the camel's back. Licinius lost his patience.

Rome was lauding only Constantine and this did not sit well with Licinius. The economic situation in the Roman Empire was improving rapidly. Measures taken by Constantine were having a good effect. He had removed taxes again for Romans, reduced them for the others and trade had flourished fast. The flow of food, wheat, olive oil and fruit across the Mediterranean from Egypt restarted. Building projects were started everywhere. Nice churches were built. People seemed happier. The number of Christians was increasing rapidly.

The Senate decided to go ahead with its project and reward Constantine for his success. An arch would be dedicated to him.

The arch had been started by Maxentius for himself, trying to present himself as "Unconquered Prince", whose divine companion was Mars Invictus, after his victories over his two imperial rivals, Severus and Galerius.

Constantine had his arch decorated with sculptures taken from earlier monuments. This saved the time and expense of carving new panels. Also, he had the recent example of Diocletian's New Arch, erected just a decade before, which employed reliefs from Claudian or Antonine structure.

The senate made sure that before it was dedicated, the monument could be considered nothing other than the Arch of Constantine by placing a clear dedicatory inscriptions on both north and south faces of it.

"To Emperor Flavius Constantinus Maximus. Father of the fatherland, and his following at one and the same time. The Senate and the Roman people have dedicated this arch to him, made proud by triumphs. With divine instigation and the might of his intelligence, together with his army, he took revenge by just arms on the tyrant."

Licinius could not put up with this situation any longer. It was war he wanted and not peace. He started looking for the right moment to strike. He was looking for a strategy as well. But he did not want to act openly. He wanted to do everything secretly, to catch Constantine by surprise.

In the winter of 315-316 it became apparent that Constantine would have a second child after all. On 7 August 316, in Arles, a son was born whom Faustia and Constantine named Constantius. Licinius immediately discerned that Bassianus could not become ceasar. Constantine would not allow it. Bassianus had ceased to be an asset to Constantine. He was instead a threat to the succession of his sons.

Licinius made a plan with Bassanius and persuaded him to do his bidding. Bassanius had to aim at the throne of the West. Senicio, Bassianus" brother who was loyal to Licinius too, became his partner in the plot.

The two brothers, Bassianus and Senicio revolted against Constantine. They discussed their plans together and imagined that the affair would turn out to their satisfaction; and now they began to speak openly of that which hitherto they had only mentioned below their breath. They had to take up arms against Constatine.

A Christian man by the name of Matthew overheard their talk. He was an Illyrian by descent, tribune in rank, who had long been attached to Emperor Constantine and counted among his faithful friends. Consequently Matthew stole out during the middle watch of the night and ran to Constantine in Arles, to report everything he had heard. Constantine gave ear to his abominable news. He immediately made preparations for a confrontation.

Heading to Arles where Constantine was residing, Bassianius judged it necessary to execute the plan to capture the throne of the West as quickly as possible. With his army he occupied Turin. He talked to Alexander, the leader of the town, and requested more soldiers, promising rewards if he succeeded in his plan to capture the throne.

"We have to give it a try. This is the prerogative of high-souled men. Soon, we will be rulers of the West," Bassianius told him.

Alexander listened to it all and seeing that such circumstances admitted of no delay, but that some drastic step had to be taken at once, said, "When to-morrow's dawn breaks, and you leave this city I will follow you with all my men and fight willingly on your side. We have to act fast, before someone goes to the Emperor and denounces you and your followers."

"As I see that you really care for my success, I shall not reject your counsel. Tomorrow we start our march towards Arles," Bassianus said.

They both exchanged assurances with oaths to the effect that if Sol Invicturs raised Bassianus to the Imperial throne, he should raise Alexander to the rank of Caesar, which he himself held in the meantime.

As they started their march towards Arles, they ran into another friend of theirs, Plautus. Plautus was already full of warlike frenzy and when they told him of their intentions, Plautus immediately agreed.

"You will always find me courageous, but more especially so when I am braving danger for high power and gold," Plautus told them.

As the army of Bassianus was camping close to a river, an army created by Constantine who had been alerted of Bassianus revolt, sourrounded them.

Bassianus was seized while still preparing himself. Alexander and Plautus were killed. Senicia escaped and went to Licinius.

Bassianus confessed that he had been pushed by Licinius and his brother Senicia to go to war with him. At Constantine's order, Bassianus was tried, convicted and executed. When Senicia, as one of the people responsible for the plot, was demanded for punishment, Licinius refused to hand him over.

The peace between the Emperors was broken.

***

Licinius learned about the fate of Bassianus from Senicia and became livid that his plan had failed miserably.

He understood that people in the West were devoted to Constantine. He tried to find out why, as Constantine now was to become his deadly enemy, and he needed to know his enemy. Licinius was told that people under Constantine's rule said that they loved him because he outshone others in courage and intelligence. They also loved him because he was exceptionally generous and very ready to give. He did not care much for riches. He gave in proportion to his wealth and he was a cheerful giver. They also said that Constantine was graced with all the virtues. For these reasons they were happy he was on the throne. They said that Constantine stood for the truth, the rule of law, individual rights, against those who persecute Christians, and prosperity for all.

"I can't compete with that. My values are different. I have to destroy him," Licinius resolved.

It became clear to Licinius that Christians were in Constantine's heart and they respected him. Constantine had been focusing on improving the situation for Christians.

Not only could they worship freely, but all churches and property seized by Diocletian was returned to them.

Constantine's Family members were converted too.

"As Christians are supporters of Constantine they will pay a heavy price for this. They are a fifth column for Constantine in my territory as well. I have to persecute them," Licinius said to himself.

Pagan priests supported Licinius.

Persecution of Christians started all across the East of the Roman Empire again. Soldiers burned their books and churches. They tortured Christians, put them in prison, and even killed many of them.

When Constantine heard of this he was saddened. The persecution of Christians and Licinius' refusal to hand over Senicia were clear signs that Licinius wanted war. There was no need for another casus belli.

***

The two Augusti prepared their armies and led them for a confrontation. The armies met in battle for the first time, in the plain of Cibalae, on October 316.
Licinius had 35 thousand men, infantry and cavalry; Constantine commanded 20 thousand foot and horse. After an indecisive battle, in which 20 thousand of Licinius' infantry and part of his armored cavalry were killed, Licinius escaped under cover of darkness to Sirmium, his capital, with the greater part of his horse. From there, having collected his wife and son and his treasury, he went to Dacia.
He made Valens, commander of the frontier, a Caesar. Then, when a huge force was gathered by Valens at Adrianople, he sent ambassadors to Constantine, who had established himself at Philippopolis, to discuss peace. The ambassadors returned frustrated, and having resumed war they fought again on the plain of Arda.
After a long and indecisive battle, Licinius" men gave way and fled in the darkness. Licinius and Valens turned away towards Berroea, believing that Constantine would pursue them by heading further towards Byzantium, which would be the wrong direction. But they were mistaken. Constantine's army followed them towards Berroea. So when Constantine was forging ahead eagerly, he caught up with them. Just then, when Licinius' soldiers were weary with battle and the forced march, Mestrianus was sent to Constantine as an ambassador to sue for peace, at the request of Licinius who promised henceforth to do as he was told. He would not persecute Christians anymore and he would agree to other terms Constantine had decided.
Valens was commanded to return to his former rank. Licinius held provinces of Oriens, Asia, Thrace, Lesser Moesia and Scythia.
A period of peace dominated in the Roman Empire.

***

Some years passed. Constantine's zeal and heart for Christianity grew. Above all he admired the giving spirit of the Christian God and Christians. "It is more blessed to give than to receive" was something he valued greatly. So Constantine decided to do something special about this. He decided to build a magnificent Church in Rome, in honor of St. Peter, which would be the Christian center of the Latin speaking Roman Empire.
The building started in 318.
Because it was going to become a major place of pilgrimage in Rome, Constantine went to great pains to build the basilica on the site of Saint Peter's grave, and this fact influenced the layout of the building. The Vatican Hill, on the west bank of the Tiber River, was leveled. The custom was to offer Mass facing eastward. This meant that popes offering Mass in the basilica faced the congregation.

The plan was for the church to be capable of housing from 3,000 to 4,000 worshipers at one time. It consisted of five aisles, a wide central nave and two smaller aisles to each side, which were each divided by 21 marble columns, taken from earlier pagan buildings. It was over 110 m long, built in the shape of a Latin cross, and had a gabled roof which was timbered on the interior and which stood at over 30 m at the center.

The exterior however, unlike earlier pagan temples, was not lavishly decorated.

The altar of Old St. Peter's Basilica used several Solomonic columns. Constantine took these columns from the Temple of Solomon and gave them to the church.

Constantine gave the church to his Christian friend Lactantius who had lost his church in Nikomedia years ago, when Diocletian had destroyed it. He had always provided help and guidance to Constantine throughout his life, and he had succeeded in all his plans. It was now time for Constantine to do something nice for Lactantius. Lactantius was very happy and grateful for this.

***

As Constantine decided to start a new big holiday for Christians, pagan priests informed Licinius of the change. Constantine had decided to declare Dec. 25, 323, the "Day of the Sun", which was celebrated by pagans, as the "Day of Birth of Christ" as well.

Stirred by pagan priests, Licinius started persecuting all Christians again.

Soon after that, war broke out once again between Licinius and Constantine.

At the end of 323, Constantine prepared for war at Salonica, which he had annexed from Licinius in 317. Formerly the capital of Galerius, it had an imperial residence and hippodrome for Constantine's immediate use. It also had a splendid natural harbor, which Constantine augmented. There, he constructed his fleet as well.

The assault was to be by land and sea, for Licinius was now based on the Sea of Marmara, shuttling between Nicomedia and the city of Byzantium.

While based at Salonica, Constantine dealt with an invasion across the Danube in spring 324 by an army of Sarmatians, led by Rausimodus, who plundered Moesia and Thrace, taking many captives. He had been encouraged by Licinius to fight against Constantine.

"Perhaps this is opportunism. Rausimodus may know of the breach between you and Licinius. Or perhaps Rausimodus has been encouraged by Licinius himself to raid our territory," Crispus said to his father Constantine.

"We have to crush the Sarmatians in battle. We have to march to repel the invasion," Constantine said.

Constantine's army swiftly moved on to Campona in Pannonia. Constantine contemplated remaining there for some time, and therefore had the walls of the castle fixed and stored the imperial tent and all the baggage inside it and placed his troops inside of it.

Then Rausimodus and the Sarmatians in their turn advanced on Campona, but on hearing that the Emperor had already taken possession of the town, they crossed River Danube running through the plain somewhere near this town and fixed their palisades between the river and the town. They managed to encircle the town, and the Emperor was cut off inside.

When night descended, and all soldiers and animals slept, Constantine could not close his eyes. The whole night long he lay awake, revolving schemes for overcoming the Sarmatians' daring by craft.

Campona was a fortified town situated on a fairly steep hill and the entire barbarian army was bivouacking down below in the plain. Constantine's forces were insufficient to allow him of attempting a pitched battle against the overwhelming numbers of the adversary.

After a long and sleepless night, Constantine came up with a solution. He put a group of soldiers close to the walls of the castle. He armed them with balls of stones of fire and burning pitch and big stones and he had a plan how to bring enemy soldiers close to the walls

In the morning he armed himself and got the army ready and led out his soldiers from the gates and placed them in full view of the enemy. Constantine placed the Roman troops just on that side of the wall where the soldiers were prepared to attack with fire, and the bulk of the opposing army was straight opposite them.

Then Constantine stood in the middle of the army and explained to the soldiers that, when the trumpet sounded the attack, they were to dismount and march forward slowly against the foe and by using mostly their arrows and javelins to provoke the Sarmatians to the attack; and as soon as they saw them drawn on and urging on their horses to the attack, they were to turn hastily and in fleeing, wheel off a little to the right and left and thus open to the enemy a clear path for coming close up to the walls. The men on the walls then would attack with balls of stone and fire.

All this was carried out according to the Emperor's orders. The Sarmatian horsemen raised their barbaric shouts, jeers and insults and hurled themselves in a body upon Constantine's lines who were marching slowly towards them, the Emperor alone being on horseback. Then Roman soldiers according to Constantine's plan drew back step by step and, pretending to retreat, unexpectedly split into two parts as if opening a very wide entrance for the enemy into the town. Directly the Sarmatians had entered this gap of the two parts of Constantine's army, the balls of stone and fire came tumbling down. Each ball over the high wall, ejected from catapults, came hurtling down into the midst of the Sarmatian cavalry with tremendous impetus.

Partly owing to the strength of catapult and partly because they gained further momentum from the sloping nature of the ground, the balls fell upon the barbarians with terrific force and crushed them on every side, mowing down, soldiers and horses. And no matter where the balls hit the horses, they forced them to sink down on the side they had received the blow and consequently to throw their riders. Many Sarmatians fell one after another in great numbers, and Constantine's men charged them from both sides; the battle pressed terribly on the Sarmatians from all sides, some were killed by the flying arrows, others wounded by spears, and most of the rest were forced into the river by the violent impact of the stone balls and there swam across or drowned.

The next day when Constantine saw the Sarmatian survivors preparing for battle again, and noticed that his own men were full of courage, he bade them get ready. He himself donned his armor and, after arranging the order of battle, descended to the slope. There he drew up his lines face to face with the Sarmatians and halted in order to join battle. He himself held the center of the line. A fierce sword fight ensued.

The Romans carried off the victory and then pursued the fleeing Sarmatians hotly. When the Emperor saw that they were pursuing them for a long distance, he was afraid that they might suddenly fall into an ambush and then, not only would the flight of the Sarmatians stop, but those who were fleeing would unite with the ambush and inflict a severe blow on the Roman army. The Emperor therefore kept riding up to his men and urging them to draw rein and breathe their horses. In this way the two armies parted that day, Rausimodus and the Sarmatians fled and Constantine, the brilliant victor and his army returned joyfully to his camp.

Rausimodus lost many soldiers and retreated back across the Danube, to get more reinforcements. He was imagining that Constantine would return to Salonica after his victory. This was not the case. The next day, when Constantine heard that Rausimodus could get more reinforcements and attack again, he set off in pursuit and crossed the Danube himself the next day. As the barbarians were fleeing towards a thickly wooded hill he attacked them and killed many of them, including Rausimodus himself. He took many prisoners, accepted the surrender of the multitude of those remaining and returned to his quarters in Campona with a throng of captives.

The Sarmatians who did not fight and those who surrendered sued for peace and pledged allegiance to Constantine. Their requests were honored. Constantine then decided that he ought to return to Salonica, in order to give himself and the larger part of his army some rest after their heavy fighting. So he divided his forces and selected the bravest of the troops to remain on guard against the enemy. Over these he placed as commanders, Illyrian brothers John and Peter Valona. He ordered them to post an adequate number of soldiers as garrison in each town, and to requisition foot-soldiers from all the country together with wagons and the oxen which drew them.

Constantine started his journey towards Salonica with a throng of captives. After distributing these among many cities, he came to the Imperial Palace in Salonica.

Unhappy about the defeat of Sarmatians, Licinius sent envoys who asserted that in repelling the Sarmatians, Constantine had violated the border between their lands in Thrace.

Constantine knew that now Licinius would attack again with all his army.

Licinius sent orders across the eastern Mediterranean that warships be sent to the Hellespont. He assembled 350 triremes, as well as 150 thousand infantry and 15 thousand cavalry.

After receiving intelligence about Licinius move, Constantine immediately ordered two hundred triremes to be built, and more than two thousand transport ships to be made available, where one hundred and twenty thousand infantry and ten thousand each of sailors and Cavalry were assembled.

***

It became obvious that the war between Constantine and Licinius would continue on a larger scale and therefore both made suitable provision and preparations beforehand.

"I did not want this war with Licinius," Constantine said to Bishop Lactantius.

"Licinius, like Maxentius and Maximinus Daia before him, is a tyrant. He wallows in avarice, cruelty and lust, murdering rich men and seducing their wives. Like the other tyrants too, he is a persecutor of Christians and deserving of divine punishment. God has chosen you as his instrument Constantine. You have to fight against Licinius," Lactantius told Constantine.

Constantine was convinced. He had to fight for his God and had to defend Christians.

The first engagement took place on July 3 and 4, 324, between Constantine's land troops and those Licinius had assembled at Adrianople in Thrace, his westernmost staging post.

Constantine sent a large force into the wooded hills above the river Hebrus. Licinius army was camped in a field behind the river. With a small number of soldiers, Constantine feigned an attack across the river, personally leading them. Surprised by the attack, Licinius asked the bugler to sound the alarm and ordered the troops to attack.

When they saw the cavalry of Licinius" army go for the bait, the small army of Constantine retreated. Encouraged, Licinius" cavalry crossed the river and continued to pursue Constantine and his small army. But they were ambushed and then killed. Using the horses of their enemies, Constantine's troops crossed the river and attacked Licinius infantry. Licinius managed to escape with a good number of his infantry but he left 34,000 killed soldiers behind.

Licinius" remaining forces withdrew in confusion towards Byzantium.

A second engagement took place at sea, in the narrow straits of the Hellespont. Off the coast of Callipolis, Constantine's ships commanded by his first son Crispus met those under Licinius' admiral Amandus.

Admiral Amandus was glad at first that Constantine was not leading these troops against him but his advisers explained to him that Crispus was a great admiral too. With 300 ships and thousands of soldiers aboard, he had often traveled the sea, mainly for trade reasons, selling clothes and wheat and olive oil in different places of the Roman Empire. He often would go on missions to preserve the peace in the seas when pirates would attack traders" vessels, to save them. He knew what the best action and decision had to be taken while at sea. He knew the sea like the back of his hand.

Amandus heeded the warning of his advisers and took all the necessary measures.

The narrowness of the strait of Callipolis persuaded Crispus to send forward only eighty ships, and in response, sensing a chance to surround and crush his enemy, Amandus sailed forth with two hundred. But with no room to maneuver, Amandus" triremes proved to be easy targets for Crispus, whose ships attacked at the right time.

Many were wrecked, and the crews of others leapt overboard abandoning their vessels. The battle continued on the following day. As the fleets re-engaged, Crispus sensed the favor of God, his father's patron. After Amandus had passed Callipolis and was directing his course to Byzantium, he was suddenly caught in a most terrible storm off the promontory. For a heavy fall of hail and rain and the winds rushing down from the mountains churned up the sea violently. Then the waves rose and roared and the oars of the rowers were broken off as they dipped them; the winds and hail tore the sails to shreds; the yard-arms were snapped off and fell on the deck, and the boats, crews and all, sank and soldiers died in the water.

Amandus' men were naturally all much disturbed and agitated and quite helpless to cope with such enemies. There was a frightful tumult, for men wailed and shrieked, called upon their god to save them, and prayed to be allowed to see the dry land. The storm did not lessen meanwhile. It was as if God were pouring out his wrath upon Licinius's men, insolent and overweening presumptuousness, and showing him from the very start that the issue would not go on his favor. Some of the ships were lost, crews and all, others were dashed on the rocks and broken to pieces. Many hides covering the turrets became stretched by the rain, so that the nails fell out of their holes and the weight of the bides soon dragged down the wooden turrets which in their fall swamped the ships.

However, the boat which carried Amandus was saved with difficulty, though badly battered; and some of the freight-ships with all on board were also miraculously saved. The sea threw up many of the men and quite a number of pouches and other oddments which the sailors had taken with them and scattered them over the shore.

The survivors buried the dead with due rites, and consequently they became infected with the horrible stench, as it was not easy for them to bury so many quickly. Now all the provisions had been lost and probably the survivors would have died of starvation, had there not been a luxuriance of crops and fruits in the fields and gardens.

Now the proportion of the loss was plain to all right-minded persons, but none of these occurrences daunted Licinius, for he was quite fearless and only prayed to Sol Invictus to allow of his fighting against his chosen enemies one more time.

Licinius was like a wounded beast, ready to fight even harder against his adversary. And so with the remaining troops which had escaped from the peril, he started preparations to form another army in Byzantium. Here he stayed so that he and the other survivors from the storm at sea might recuperate, and that those he had left behind at Callipolis and others, whom he expected to come by sea from Nikomedia and other places, might join him, as well as the troops who had started overland a short time before, the fury-equipped cavalry, infantry and the light-armed soldiers. When he had collected his whole army from land and sea, he stayed in Byzantium with all his troops.

It was not long before Constantine's army showed up before the walls of Byzantium.

***

As Constantine's men raised a mound against the walls and rolled forward their siege engines, Licinius abandoned Byzantium during the night, leaving it in the hands of the inhabitants there and sailed to Chalcedon.

There he secured the support of an army of Goths, led by Alica, which joined his line. Despite his failure to hold Byzantium and his lost ships, the advantage was once again with him, the older Augustus. He had a greater number of troops than Constantine.

Licinius arrayed his forces on the hills above Chalcedon and sent the captain of his court guard, Martinianus, to nearby Lamsakos, to prevent Crispus' ships from ferrying Constantine's army across.

To induce Martinianus to remain loyal, Licinius promoted him to the rank of Ceasar, just as he had his expendable subordinate Valens in 316.

Constantine avoided the trap by leaving his transport ships at Callipolis and swiftly building new skiffs and barges and requisitioning those anchored nearby, he sailed across the Hellespont at the mouth of the Black Sea to Hieron, the 'sacred Promontory", two hundred roman stades north of Chalcedon.

There Constantine landed his army and went up to some hills from which he extended his battle line.

Licinius saw that Bithynia was now in enemy hands, yet having been thoroughly tested in all dangers he recalled Martinianus from Lampsakos and encouraged his men by promising them solemnly that he would command them himself and give rich lands to them after the victory.

He then drew up his army and advanced from Chalcedon to Hieron. But during the battle there, Constantine won convincingly, for he attacked the enemy vigorously and effected such carnage that barely thirty thousand escaped.

Licinius withdrew from the battlefield to Nicomedia his last resort, with his remaining forces: those not killed in the several encounters, or taken captive, or who had not fled or deserted.

Meanwhile Constantine, entirely freed from anxiety, collected all the booty and the Imperial tent, and, with these trophies and with much exultation, settled down again in a plain close to Hieron. After a short rest he began to consider whether he ought to make another attempt on Chrysopolis" walls, or postpone the siege while lodging all his troops in the sequestered vales that lie between Chalcedon and Hieron. Constantine sent envoys to Chrysopolis and asked them to surrender.

***

After hearing what the envoys had to say, the inhabitants of Chrysopolis, the majority of whom were colonists from Rome and Venice, on hearing of the Emperor Licinius" misfortune, and the terrible carnage, and the death of so many of his men and the ruin of his fleet and Constantine's intention of starting a siege of their city, they began individually to deliberate what action they had better take to ensure their safety and not incur more risks on their heads. Consequently they called an assembly where they openly stated their private opinions and after discussing the vital points they thought they had found the only path, as it were, out of a labyrinth, which was to decide to listen to Constantine and surrender the city to him.

One of the Illyrian colonists from Scodra, still further incited them to this course, so they allowed themselves to be persuaded by his arguments, and threw open the gates and gave Constantine entrance. After taking possession, he sent for the troops and dividing them according to race, enquired of each soldier individually whether he had been seriously wounded or had perhaps received a slight scratch from a sword; at the same time he found out how many and what class of men had fallen in the preceding battles. And, during that month, he intended to reinforce his troops, and at the first opportunity to march against Emperor Licinius with his whole army. However, Constantine was not alone in formulating such plans, although everybody congratulated him on being the victor and winning the trophies. He always took in consideration other generals" thoughts and ideas.

Emperor Licinius, worsted and badly wounded, was scared and much depressed by his intolerable defeat and the loss of so many brave soldiers.

Now that he had made much experience of Constantine and the boldness of his large army, Licinius blamed all the defeat to his generals. He condemned his own leaders for great negligence and cowardice.

He thought he needed other allies and more mercenaries. But how was he to get them without money? For there was none in his Imperial Treasury which had been depleted so thoroughly by continuous wars. The gates of the treasure-house were not even locked now, but carelessly left open for anyone who liked to walk through them; for all its contents had been squandered.

What an embarrassment for the Roman state of the East, which was oppressed simultaneously by weakness and poverty, at a time when the Western Part was strong and prosperous.

And all the cities had fallen in the hands of Constantine one after another. Nikodemia was the only city standing. And it was not long before Constantine's army laid a siege of it.

This was the moment when Emperor Licinius decided to give up fighting. He did not care any longer of doing things unworthy of, or inconsistent with, his own military knowledge and bravery. He focused his attention on one point. Peace.

His wife Constantia, Constantine's half sister, was the only card that Licinius could play now. He did not hesitate.

He immediately requested his wife to seek peace with Constantine. He explained the situation to her. He told her the truth that he had been hiding from her.

He told Constantia that he had too few men to resist, and he had decided to surrender and he needed her help. Constantia was shocked at the news but she promised she would do everything to help him.

Licinius asked her to go to Constantine and beg for his life.

Constantia went and she persuaded her brother.

When what she requested was granted, Licinius came in person to relinquish his purple cloak.

Constantine forgave him and allowed him to go and live in Salonica as a private citizen.

Constantine sent Licinius to Salonica, but people there hated him so much for the great carnage he had done in the past. He had persecuted and killed their loved ones. To them he was only a tyrant and God-hater. And so they murdered him in the spring of 325. Such was the fate of many other of his collaborators. It was divine justice. Martinianus was tracked down and killed in Cappadocia.

Constantia, was treated with remarkable clemency, because of her blood ties to Constantine. She became a Christian.

To mark his victory in a war he had fought and to restore toleration, Constantine issued a statement to his newest subjects.

"My own desire, for the common good of the world and the advantage of all mankind, is that people should enjoy a life of peace and undisturbed concord.

Let those, therefore, who still delight in error, be made welcome to the same degree of peace and tranquility that is enjoyed by those who believe. For it may be that this restoration of equal privileges to all will prevail to lead them onto the straight path.

Let no one molest another, but let everyone do as his soul desires.

Only let men of sound judgment be assured of this, that those only can live a life of holiness and purity, whom God calls to a reliance on His holy laws.

With regard to those who will hold themselves aloof from us, let them have, if they please, their temples of lies.

We have the glorious edifice of God's truth, which He has given us as our native home.

We pray, however, that they too may receive the same blessing, and thus experience that heartfelt joy which unity of sentiment inspires."

#

CHAPTER 10

CONSTANTINE, THE SOLE EMPEROR OF ROME

WHILE CONSTANTINE and Lactantius were still in Nicomedia preparing to leave for Rome, they happened to see the place where the Christian Church once stood, which Diocletian had destroyed.

"You know what Diocletian said after my church was destroyed?" Lactantius told Constantine.

"No, Lactantius. But I know that you almost got killed by Diocletian's soldiers. And I heard that believers in your church saved your life," said Constantine.

"Yes, they did save my life," admitted Lactantius.

"So what did Diocletian say?"

"Diocletian said that Jesus Christ is homeless again," Lactantius said.

"It sounds just like him. We will rebuild this church and many others throughout the Empire Lactantius. You don't have to worry about this. Jesus is never going to be homeless again in the Roman Empire. I promise," Constantine said as a great desire to express his gratitude to God filled his heart.

Lactantius knew that Constantine meant what he said. He had no doubt that when Constantine promised something, he would do it.

As they approached the port, Constantine and Lactantius met with Crispus and the Roman army, boarded their ships and returned to Italy through the Mediterranean Sea. When they reached Rome and were riding in its streets, crowds of people cheered and threw flowers at victorious Constantine and his army.

Constantine had become the sole Emperor of the Roman Empire.

He immediately took the same measures in the East as he had taken in the West in regards to toleration of Christianity. In fact, he put his full force of favor towards advancing the cause of the Church of Christ. He provided Christianizing legislation on the observance of Sunday, making it an official Roman holiday. He returned property and treasures to all Christian churches, and exempted some clergy from taxes. He also funded some Christian leaders and the construction of churches which had been destroyed by Diocletian, Galerius or Licinius. Most Christian leaders greatly admired Constantine for the works he was doing for the church and Christian cause.

Christianity in the East flourished in as many ways as in the West. Followers were now safe from persecution. Christian leaders were frequently given many gifts by the Emperor himself. Constantine's adherence to Christianity ensured exposure of all his subjects to the religion in the Roman Empire, and this was no small domain.

The Roman Empire reached its territorial, political and spiritual peace and unity after a long period of civil wars. Western and Eastern Roman Empire celebrated Christmas together for the first time in their history. And on top of all this, Constantine started building a new Rome, a new city dedicated to God, so the Eastern Greek-speaking citizens had a place of pilgrimage of their own.

✦✦✦

Despite the measures taken, the situation especially among Eastern Christian churches was not as good as Constantine wished. There was a controversy among the nature of Christ that was creating many problems among Christians. Some Christians declared that Christ was just a man. Others, which constituted the great majority said that he was more than a man, that he was divine, equal to the Father in every way. This controversy needed to be sorted out one way or another as a house divided could not stand.

When he talked to Bishop Lactantius, Constantine asked him for a solution.

Lactantius had thought about this problem and told him about a meeting of bishops to solve the problem by coming up with a creed of the Christian faith.

"Bishops need to come up with a creed that will be used by Christians now and in the centuries to come," Lactantius said. "We need to organize a big meeting, a council of all the Bishops for this," he added.

Constantine became pensive for a moment. This seemed like a good idea to him.

"I will provide all that is necessary for this meeting. We need to solve this problem because it's dividing Christians and causing much tension and strife in the Empire. I don't know where we can hold this meeting though because the church of Rome has not been completed yet. Do you have any suggestions Lactantius?" Constantine asked.

"The church in Rome can't be used because it is being rebuilt. Nicea has a big church which can be used for this purpose. It is also closer to all the churches. We can invite all Bishops all over the world as long as you will provide for their travel and lodging and food," said Lactantius.

"It will be my pleasure! Whoever can come is welcome in the meeting," Constantine said without hesitation.

Lactantius was always amazed with Constantine's generosity. He was very happy about this last decision. The meeting would be a great show of unity and harmony between Christians of all races and ethnicities in the world, worshiping the true God. He went home and wrote the invitation to all bishops to meet in Nicea at the very beginning of June. Copies were made by copiers and they were delivered to all the Bishops across the world through imperial couriers. 1800 invitations were sent to bishops in the east and west, across the Roman Empire, and in all those places of the world where the Christian church had been established.

In the middle of May, Constantine and Lactantius were the first to travel to Nicea to host the bishops.

Unfortunately, not all of the Bishops were able to make it to the meeting. The number of Bishops was a little over 300 at the beginning of June. But these Bishops had not traveled alone. Each had permission to bring with them two Priests and three Deacons. So the total number of attendees in the end was over 1800. It was a beautiful sight to see this host of believers gather in Nicea from all around the world. Among their midst, one could see seriousness and excitement about the meeting.

Lactantius talked with many of the Bishops before the meeting started, as he was the one who greeted all of them. He already knew some of the Bishops, such as, Eusebius of Caesarea, Athanasius of Alexandria, Eustathius of Antioch, Socrates Scholasticus, Evangrius, Hilary of Poitiers, Jerome, Dionysius, Exiguus, Rufinus. He also got to know others, like Macarius of Jerusalem, Paphnutius of Thebes, Potamon of Heraclea and Paul of Neocaesarea, Aristakes of

Armenia, Leontius of Caesarea, Hypatius of Gangra, Protogenes of Sardica, Melitius of Sebastopolis, Achilleus of Larissa.

Some of the Bishops told him very interesting stories about their life and work for the Lord.

Jacob of Nisibis had formerly been a hermit.

Spyridion of Trimythous made his living as a shepherd while he worked as a Bishop at the same time and cared for the flock of God.

Some of the Bishops came from foreign places, not the Roman Empire. John was the Bishop of Persia and India at the same time. Theophilus was a Bishop of Goths. Stratophilus was the Bishop of Georgia.

At least five representatives came from the Latin-speaking provinces, Marcus of Calabria from Italia, Cecilian of Carthage from Africa, Hosius of Córdoba from Hispania, Nicasius of Die from Gaul, and Domnus of Stridon from the province of the Danube.

Some of the supporters of Arius expressed their views openly before the meeting started but they were keeping an open mind to what others had to say. Among these were Secundus of Ptolemais, Theonus of Marmarica, Zphyrius, and Dathes, all of whom hailed from the Libyan Pentapolis. Other supporters included Eusebius of Nicomedia, Paulinus of Tyrus, Actius of Lydda, Menophantus of Ephesus, and Theognus of Nicaea.

In their conversations with Lactantius, all Bishops agreed on the importance of the Council of Nicea because it would decide on matters that would bring peace among Christians, and avoid problems that had been created in the past.

Moreover, all said that they had attached a special prominence because the persecution of Christians had just ended with the enforcement of the Edict of Milan in the East of the Roman Empire. That had changed many things. A new chapter had started. Christians were no longer considered as second class citizens in the East or anywhere else in the Roman Empire. They now had equal rights to others.

The signs of persecution which had happened in the past could be seen on the faces of many Bishops. Big scars in the shape of a cross were sad reminders of the cruelty of former Emperors of Rome.

Soon the Bishops agreed on the day that the Council of Nicea be held in the big and beautiful Church of the city. It was to be on the first Sunday of June.

It was a nice and sunny day when the Bishops started to gather in the Church that Sunday. They all got seated in the pews and waited for the Emperor to join them. They did not wait long. Resplendent in purple and gold, accompanied by a few imperial Praetorian guards, Constantine made a ceremonial entrance at the opening of the council. He proceeded through the midst of the assembly. The respect of all the Bishops was great. As soon as they saw him, they got up, turned towards him and started to applaud the Emperor who had done so much for Christianity.

Clothed in raiment which glittered as with rays of light, reflecting the glowing radiance of a purple robe, and adorned with the brilliant splendor of gold and precious stones, Constantine walked calmly between the two main isles of the church and seated himself in a throne at the head of the Church. He was there only as an overseer and presider only.

The council was organized along the lines of the Roman Senate. Hosius of Cordoba presided over the deliberations. Eusebius of Nicomedia delivered the welcoming address to all the Bishops.

Then the Bishops started their discussions and debates. Many of them spoke up and expressed their views on what the teaching of the Bible was regarding Jesus Christ. As it was hard to decide just through discussions, it was decided that the matter would be decided by votes. And that's what happened. Votes were cast on the issue, to see what the general view of all the Bishops was.

When the result of the voting was checked, it became clear that the great majority of the Bishops thought that the teaching of the Bible was that Jesus was divine, the Son of God, equal to the Father.

After the result became public Bishops stood up and applauded. Then they decided to create a committee to come up with the Creed of Faith for which they had gathered. When the committee presented the draft of the Creed the Bishops were happy. The Council of Nicea approved the Creed. The meeting had reached its purpose. It came out with one Creed of Faith for all Christians of all times. The Bishops left Nicea with the words of the Creed which they sent to all their congregations.

"We believe in one God, the Father, Almighty, Maker of all things visible and invisible; and in the one Lord Jesus Christ, the Son of God, begotten of the Father, only-begotten, that is, from the substance of the Father; God from God, Light from Light, Very God from Very God, begotten not made, of one substance with the Father, through whom all things were made, both in heaven and in earth; who for us men and for our salvation came down and was incarnate, was made man, suffered, and rose again on the third day, ascended into heaven, and is coming to judge the living and the dead; And in the Holy Spirit. And those who say: "There was a time when he was not," and: "Before he was begotten he was not," and: "He came into being from nothing," or those who pretend that the Son of God is "of another substance" than the Father or "created" or "alterable" or "mutable," the catholic and apostolic church places under a curse."

#

CHAPTER 11

FAMILY TROUBLES IN THE IMPERIAL PALACE

AFTER THE COUNCIL OF NICEA, Constantine and Lactantius headed to the Imperial Palace of Arles, where Fausta had gone to meet with her parents. Constantine invited Lactantius for lunch.

Fausta welcomed them when they arrived at the Palace. The servants brought food for the Emperor and Empress and their guest Lactantius.

Constantine and Lactantius were happy with the result of the meeting. They gave thanks to God for what had happened in Nicea before they started eating. And then they started talking about family issues.

"Your husband, the Emperor, is the best Roman Emperor ever! He has done great things for the Roman Empire and for Christians in particular" Lactantius said to Fausta.

"We have three sons and two daughters together. They all admire and adore him so much. I hope and pray that his sons and daughters will follow in his footsteps and become great like him," said Fausta.

"Their half-brother Crispus has become a great man too," said Lactantius.

"That's true," Constantine interjected. "Without him I could not have won against Licinius. He is a great General. You should have seen him fighting. He is very brave. I am sure that my first wife, Minervina, would have been very proud of him, if she were still alive, to see him as a Caesar, and when I am gone, as an Emperor," Constantine said.

"Where is he now," asked Lactantius.

"He is in charge of some areas which Bassanius controlled, before he betrayed us and got his right punishment. After Bassanius was killed, I put Crispus as a Caesar in his place and he did not disappoint me because when I needed his help in my fight against Licinius, he was there. His help was invaluable. I am very grateful to him," said Constantine.

"Do you see him sometimes?" asked Lactantius.

"Once in a while," said Constantine. Fausta nodded her head.

"He comes and tells us what he is doing?" Fausta added.

"But he is a grown-up and I am glad he can now stand on his own," Constantine added. "He reminds me of myself when I was young, and of his mother, Minervina, whom I loved dearly," Constantine said.

Fausta looked at Constantine, not without some jealousy, that he said those words about his first wife in her presence and that of someone else. She felt like Constantine loved her less.

"I am the daughter of former Emperor Maximian. I hope you love me dearly too," said Fausta.

"I love you dearly too," said Constantine reassuring his wife.

Just then, a servant came to the table and told Fausta that her little boy was crying and was requesting to see her. Fausta excused herself and went to see the kid who was named after Constantine.

"I can't help but notice that there will certainly be some rivalry between the three sons you have with Fausta and your other son with Minervina, Crispus," said Lactantius.

"That's true. But I will arrange everything when the right time comes. All of them will have their fair share of power in the Roman Empire," Constantine said.

***

As days passed after that meeting, Fausta became increasingly concerned about the future of her three boys. What would happen to them in the future? Would they one day become Caesars and Emperors? What if things went wrong? What if Crispus did not like her sons and … and decided to do the unthinkable like all other contenders for the throne of Emperor did, harm them. Cold shivers went down Fausta's spine. Contenders did crazy things at times. Was Crispus to be trusted? Fausta could not find peace from these thoughts. She had to talk to somebody.

When Fausta opened her heart to her father, Maximian, she was surprised that he was critical of Crispus. He had no doubt that Crispus was a big problem. Something needed to be done to clarify the stance that Crispus would hold in the future. He could not bear the thought of his nephews getting outmaneuvered by an experienced general like Crispus.

Fausta talked to her mother too and she expressed the same concerns that Maximian had voiced.

"Your father Maximian who was a great Emperor is sure that Crispus will kill your children. Don't be naïve in believing that Crispus will share his power with your sons. He sees your sons as rivals, nothing else. And he will do anything, anything, to make sure that he gets all the power when your husband Constantine is gone. Crispus shall kill your sons. In fact, he may kill your husband Constantine too. Something needs to be done Fausta, sooner rather than later," her mother said.

After these disturbing conversations, Fausta began to spend too much time by herself. The more she thought about the situation, the more she was convinced that her mother was right. This was a matter of life or death for her sons. Her sons were in great danger. Not only would they not become Caesars or Emperors in the future, but they could be killed as well. And her husband Constantine was in danger too. These thoughts were becoming unbearable. Fausta felt she had to talk to her husband Constantine about this possible future development.

The words of her father and mother had convinced Fausta that Crispus was a danger to Constantine's throne, that Crispus was desperately trying to de-throne him, just as Bassanius did. That's why Crispus fought so hard against Licinius too. He wanted to become Emperor himself. So he had to get rid of Licinius too. Constantine was next. And then her dear sons.

Fausta could not wait. As soon as she got the opportunity, she talked to Constantine. She was stunned when he dismissed her ideas as nonsense. He even called her paranoid needed to calm down.

But Fausta could not. There was only one word that came back to her mind repeatedly when she thought about Crispus, "rival". Crispus was a rival to Constantine and her sons. There was no guaranty that Crispus would be nice to Constantine and her sons when so much was at stake. He was just waiting for his opportunity to strike.

Fausta went back to her parents because she could not find peace in her mind and heart. They told Fausta that they had certain information that Crispus was contemplating the assassination of Constantine. Some generals who used to work for Maximian had heard Crispus say that he would soon capture the throne. According to them, this meant that he was preparing a plot against Constantine. Fausta was shaken. She did not know what to do or think.

**

Fausta's parents told her to tell Constantine about what the generals had communicated to them. They were accusing Crispus of betrayal. Fausta did not hesitate. When Constantine returned home and was eating his lunch, she delivered him the bad news. Three generals had accused Crispus of plotting to kill him, the Emperor.

Constantine could not believe his ears. Fausta had talked to him in the past about how Crispus was a rival and a danger to him and their sons, but he had never thought that Crispus would go that far.

"Could it be?" he asked Fausta.

"I believe it," said Fausta. "They are three respected generals. They said that quick action is needed, as in the case of Bassanius, before it's too late. He and Bassanius the traitor were friends. We should do something. There's a law in our land, the Roman Empire, which says, "Guilty until proven innocent". Crispus should be arrested and held in jail until things get sorted out. Is this too much to ask?" Fausta added.

"But, how can I arrest him? He is my son. What will people say? All kinds of rumors will spread," said Constantine.

"The law is the law. You are the Emperor and you must uphold the law of the land. If not you, who will?" said Fausta.

"I want to talk with the generals," said Constantine.

Fausta went out and returned with the three generals. They all confirmed what Fausta had just said. Crispus was plotting an attack against Constantine and wanted to become the Emperor of Rome.

Constantine was not sure how reliable the testimony of these generals were and what to do next. But Fausta kept insisting that his life was in great danger and Crispus had to be arrested.

In the end, Constantine gave in. After all, the law of the land was what Fausta had said, "Guilty until proven innocent". If Crispus was innocent, he would prove that he was innocent and everything would be okay then.

Constantine signed the letter for the arrest of Crispus. When Roman soldiers arrived at Crispus' house and showed him the warrant for his arrest, he was surprised.

"This is nonsense. I am innocent. I am not planning to dethrone my father. There must be a mistake. I can prove that I am innocent. I need to talk to my father," Crispus said out loud.

"We are just doing our job Caesar. We have orders to arrest you and hold you in prison until you clear your name," the soldiers said.

Crispus did not resist. He gave himself up. The soldiers sent him to a prison in Pola of Illyria. A few days passed. The guards told Crispus that Constantine would come to see him in a couple of weeks.

Fausta was told about the arrest of Crispus and that he was sent to a prison in Pola. Prison guards there were trusted friends of former Emperor Maximian. And by his orders, as soon as he was put in prison, Crispus was poisoned.

The news that Crispus had died spread immediately.

When they told Fausta that Crispus was dead, she was surprised. Her kids were now safe but she felt guilty about his death. And she knew that sooner or later she would be accused too of killing Crispus. She had insisted on his arrest. Her conscience was not clean and she became deeply disturbed inside.

"What could happen to me? I could be arrested," she thought to herself.

She thought about the trial and all the trouble she would be facing. All the shame she and her parents had to go through. All the name-calling. All the negative attention to herself and her parents. She did not want any of that. But it was bound to happen. The more she thought about a solution, the more she was convinced that there was only one. She had to kill herself. That was a short cut, a desirable end. She had to find the courage in her heart to go through with this idea. She had to.

When Constantine learned about the death of Crispus he was shocked. He immediately requested a full report on the incident. He needed to know exactly what had happened.

When his mother Helen learnt about the death of Crispus, she immediately came for a visit. She came to console her son Constantine. She also could not believe that Crispus, the son of Minervina was dead too. She had loved both Minervina and Crispus.

Constantine explained to her what had happened, how Fausta had brought three generals who had accused Crispus of betrayal.

"You need to talk directly to Fausta," Helen said.

Constantine became pensive but said nothing for a few moments.

"You are right. I need to go and talk to Fausta," Constantine finally said to his mother.

Just as he was getting ready to leave, a messenger arrived. He delivered another shocking news. Fausta had committed suicide.

Constantine became overwhelmed with emotion. First his son and now Fausta. Two people that he loved were gone in just a short time.

It was not clear why these events had happened. People were speculating wildly about what had actually transpired. Constantine himself could not find the truth. He could only speculate too and think that all this was about rivalry among his sons. In his mind, he had clearly made plans to share power among all of his sons. He had a fair plan. But because he had been too busy with the problems of the Roman Empire, he had not been able to see this problem in his own home in time and fix it. Constantine felt guilty because he had not paid much attention to the situation. Guilt overwhelmed him. And that made him feel more in debt to God and that he needed more forgiveness and mercy.

#

CHAPTER 12

LIFE WITH GOD GOES ON

CONSTANTINE did not let the tragedy in his family distract him from his devotion to God. On the contrary, he increased his service to God.

He continued with the building of Churches and his new city in Byzantium. Whenever he received a request from bishops about new churches in their cities, he would provide as much help as he could. In this way, he helped with the construction of churches in Jerusalem, after a request of Bishop Macarius.

The Bishop wrote to him that the Roman Emperor Hadrian in the 2nd century had built a temple dedicated to the Roman goddess Venus, in order to bury the cave in which Jesus had been buried. As soon as Constantine received the message, he ordered that the temple be replaced by a church. The construction of the church started immediately.

During the building of the Church, Constantine's mother, Helena, went for a visit. She found three crosses in the sepulcher, and with them, she found the tablet of Pilate, on which he had inscribed that the Christ who was crucified was the King of the Jews. Since, however, it was doubtful which was the cross of Jesus, and which those of the thieves. The Emperor's mother did not get discouraged. She believed that the truth would somehow be revealed. And this is what happened. A woman from Jerusalem, who had been long afflicted with disease and was at the point of death, asked to see the three crosses. To fulfill her last wish, her relatives brought her to the church. She touched the three crosses one after another. When she touched the third one, a blast of energy fell upon her body and she was healed immediately. And everyone who saw what happened, including Helen, had no doubt that that was the cross of Jesus. The Emperor's mother named the new sepulcher the New Jerusalem. It stood facing the old and deserted city. There she left a portion of the cross, enclosed in a silver case, as a memorial to those who might wish to see it. The other part she sent to Constantine who enclosed it in a statue, on a large column of porphyry in his own Forum in the new city in Byzantium, which was being rebuilt.

The Emperor supplied all materials for the construction of other churches as well and he even wrote to Bishops to expedite these edifices.

Another church was built over a cave at Bethlehem where Christ was born. Another was built on the mount where Christ ascended to heaven.

After having built these churches in Jerusalem, Constantine then focused on building the new Christian Center in the East, the New Rome. Because the Roman Empire was divided more or less in two parts, the Greek-speaking and the Latin-speaking part, a Christian Center in the East was necessary.

"People have been working hard to build a new city in Byzantium since 324. Why is this new city so important to Constantine?" Eusebius of Cesarea asked Lactantius.

"Constantine is determined to establish the Christian faith in the entire Roman Empire, Eusebius. Licinius caused great damage to churches and Christians. In a symbolic sense, hi defeat represents the defeat of a rival center of Pagan and Greek-speaking political activity in the East, as opposed to the Christian and Latin-speaking Rome. Christians are now free in the East as well. The creation of this Christian center, which will also be a center of learning, prosperity, and cultural preservation gives a clear message that now there is freedom for all, especially Christians who have suffered so much from persecution," Lactantius said.

"Freedom for all, is indeed a great thing. Was Byzantium the only location proposed as the New Rome?" Eusebius asked.

"No, there were several. Among the various locations proposed for this alternative capital, Constantine considered Serdica, Sirmium and Thessalonica. Eventually, however, Constantine decided to work on the Greek city of Byzantium, which offered the advantage of having already been extensively rebuilt on Roman patterns of urbanism, during the preceding century, by Septimius Severus and Caracalla, who had already acknowledged its strategic importance," Lactantius answered.

"How long has this construction work been going on?" asked Eusebius.

"Sometimes it seems like forever," Lactantius joked. "But it's been about six years and it is finally coming to an end. The city is ready. We are going to inaugurate it soon and you are welcome to participate in this event." Lactantius said.

"I'll be there gladly," Eusebius said.

***

Eusebius came to meet with Lactantius on the inauguration day just as he promised. They both were talking a walk in the new city on May 11, 330, as people had filled the streets to celebrate this event.

"The Senate of Byzantium decided to change its name into Constantinopolis, in honor of Constantine," Lactantius said, as he saw Constantine riding in its street. Both bishops watched as people cheered him and women threw flowers at him. He was their Emperor, their leader, their hero, the founder of the new city, their champion of freedom.

"The new city looks beautiful after 6 years of construction work," Eusebius observed.

"Constantine has divided the expanded city, like Rome, into 14 regions, and ornamented it with public works worthy of an imperial metropolis. It possesses a proconsul. It has its senators, like those of Rome. The new program of building was carried out expeditiously: columns, marbles, doors, and tiles were taken from the temples of the Empire and moved to the new city. In similar fashion, many of the greatest works of Greek and Roman art appear in its squares and streets. The Emperor stimulated private building by promising householders gifts of land from the imperial estates in Asiana and Pontica. As in Rome, free distributions of food was made to the citizens, 80,000 rations a day, doled out from 117 distribution points around the city," Lactantius said.

"That's pretty amazing," Eusebius said. "No Emperor has done so much for Christians ever," he added.

"That's not all," continued Lactantius. "Constantine laid out a new square at the center of old Byzantium, and the Senate in the new senate-house named it the Augustaeum. On the south side of the great square is the Great Palace of the Emperor with its imposing entrance, the Chalke, and its ceremonial suite, the Palace of Daphne. Nearby is the vast Hippodrome for chariot-races, seating over 80,000 spectators, and the famed Baths of Zeuxippus. At the western entrance to the Augustaeum is the Milion, a vaulted monument from which distances are measured across the Eastern Roman Empire," Lactantius said.

"What is the name of this street we are treading on," Eusebius said.

"This is Mesi Udhes, the Middle Street, a street with an Illyrian name. It starts from the Augustaeum where it is lined with colonnades. As it descends the First Hill of the city and climbs the Second Hill, it passes on the left the Praetorium, the law-court. Then it passes through the oval Forum of Constantine where there is a second Senate-house and a high column with a statue of Constantine himself in the guise of Helios, crowned with a halo of seven rays and looking toward the rising sun. From there the Mesi Udhes passes on and through the Forum Tauri and then the Forum Bovis, and finally up the Seventh Hill and through to the Golden Gate in the Constantinian Wall," Lactantius said.

"I see jubilant people everywhere," said Eusebius.

"It's a great event indeed. And the Senate has already issued special commemorative coins to honor the event," Lactantius said.

"What symbolic sings are there in this city which show that it is a Christian city?" Eusebius asked.

"The new city is protected by the relics of the True Cross, the Rod of Moses and other holy relics. The figures of old gods have been mainly replaced. Some of them were assimilated into a framework of Christian symbolism. Constantine built the new Church of the Holy Apostles on the site of a temple to Aphrodite," Lactantius said.

"It seems certain that Constantople will become the New Rome of the East. I can see the big changes that have been made. It has been transformed from a city of earth to a city of marble," Eusebius said.

"I am sure it will become the New Rome," Lactantius said.

"Is Constantine going to live here?" asked Eusebius.

"Constantine considers Constantinople as his capital and permanent residence. He lives here most of the time. He rebuilt Trajan's bridge across the Danube, in hopes of reconquering Dacia, a province that was abandoned under Aurelian," Lactantius said.

"So he still has more battles to fight," Eusebius said.

"Even after building the city, Constantine has not stopped his plans and his fight for the freedom of the Roman Empire. He will continue to fight till his last breath," Lactantius said.

***

After the inauguration of Constantinople, Constantine settled in the new city. It became his new administrative seat of the Empire. Things went smoothly for a couple of years until in the late winter of 332, when the Goths attacked again. Constantine sent his son Constantius at the head of an army to repel them. The campaign of his son was a great success.

The weather and lack of food cost the Goths dearly. Nearly one hundred thousand died before they submitted to Rome. Their leader Wilhelm was captured alive.

Constantius, upon reaching Byzantium with Wilhelm, the leader of the Goths and other captured Goths, was received with honors for his victory. He was allowed to display the spoils and slaves from the war in the midst of the city and led a triumph, going on foot from his own house to the hippodrome and then again from the barriers, the starting point for the racers at the open end of the Hippodrome, until he reached the place where the imperial throne is. The spoils surprised many. Most of the articles were set apart for the royal service: thrones of gold and royal carriages and much jewelry made of precious stones, and golden drinking cups, and all the other things which are useful for the royal table. And there was also silver weighing many thousands of talents and all the royal treasure amounting to an exceedingly great sum. And there were slaves in the triumph, among whom was Wilhelm himself, wearing some sort of a purple garment upon his shoulders, and all his family, and as many of the Gothic soldiers as were very tall and muscular. And when Wilhelm reached the hippodrome and saw the Emperor sitting upon a lofty seat and the people standing on either side and realized as he looked about in what an evil plight he was, he neither wept nor cried out. And when he came before the Emperor's seat, he stripped off the purple garment, and fell prone on the ground and did obeisance to Emperor Constantine. Emperor Constantine offered peace to Wilhelm and a promise to reinstate him as a leader in his lands, if he accepted to become a friend of the Roman Empire. Wilhelm accepted and was re-instated with all previous honors.

But in 334, after Gothic commoners overthrew Wilhelm, Constantine led another campaign against them. He won a victory in the war and extended his control over the region. Constantine resettled some Sarmatian exiles as farmers in Illyrian and Roman districts, and conscripted the rest into the army. Constantine took the title Dacicus maximus in 336, during his 30th Anniversary as Emperor in a ceremony held at the Constantine's Forum.

***

Lactantius, held a speech during this event to honor his Emperor and friend Constantine. "The Emperor is and has always been the Champion of Freedom. He has fought many battles. Sometimes he overcame his adversaries by prowess. At other times he conquered by his quick wit. As I know from what his battle friends have told me, during a battle he occasionally thought out some clever device. And by daringly using it, he carried off the victory. He was excellent on using stratagems on some occasions. On others he won by hard fighting and set up numerous trophies. If there ever was a man who was fond of danger at the heat of the battle, it was he. And dangers could be seen continually rising up in his path, and at times he would walk into them bare-headed and come to close quarters with the barbarians, and at others again he would pretend to decline battle, and act the frightened man, if the occasion demanded it and circumstances advised it. One thing is certain in what he did as a general. He prevailed when he fled, and conquered when he pursued, and falling he stood, and dropping down he was erect.
Not only has he been a great General during all his reign, but also a good administrator of the Roman Empire. The economy has improved considerably. Never has the Roman Empire been richer before. Constantine restored the value of money, because it had previously been devalued by Diocletian. Moreover, his monetary policies were closely associated with his religious ones. He returned all confiscated property of churches by former Emperors, whether it was gold, land or monetary assets. He built many churches across the Empire and he built a new Rome, Constantinopolis, a new beautiful city for Christians. He well deservers our highest respect for what he has done," Lactantius concluded.
All present applauded.

***

As soon as the ceremony of his 30th Anniversary as Emperor ended, Constantine got the bad news that the Roman Empire had been attacked by the Persians again. He was talking a walk with Lactantius when a scout showed up.
"Border raids by Persians have become a usual phenomenon, Constantine. Moreover, despite the fact that you have written to Shapur II, the king of Persia, and asserted your patronage over Persia's Christian subjects and urged him to treat them well, the situation has not changed. Shapur II is persecuting Christians," a scout told Constantine.
"I have sent my 19-year-old son Constantius to guard the eastern frontier since 335," said Constantine.
"Unfortunately, things have not worked as expected, Constantine. Prince Narseh II has recently invaded Armenia, a Christian kingdom since 301. He has installed e Persian client on the throne. The Christian population there is being persecuted again," Lactantius said.
"I have to campaign against Persia myself, even though I have not been feeling well lately. This will be a Christian crusade Lactantius. Call for bishops to accompany the army. Make an imperial tent in the shape of a church to follow my army," Constantine told Lactantius.
Preparations for the campaign started feverishly.
As soldiers and weapons were being gathered from different areas of the Roman Empire, Persian diplomats came to Constantinople over the winter of 336-7, seeking peace. Because they did not accept Constantine's terms for peace, they were turned away without a deal.
Constantine's army marched towards Babylon of Persia. Cities started falling one after another. Persian diplomats came again to see Constantine and sue for peace. They accepted Constantine's terms. Christians would not be persecuted anymore.
The campaign was successful. Constantine returned victorious in Constantinople.

***

Soon after the Feast of Easter 337, Constantine fell seriously ill. As he left Constantinople, he made a voyage to Helenopolis that he might try the effect of the medicinal hot springs in the vicinity of that city on the southern shores of the Gulf of Nikomedia. Perceiving that his illness increased, he deferred the use of baths and went to a church built in honor of Lucian the Apostle. There he prayed for God's will. As he prayed, he realized that he was dying. He told Lactantius about his premonitions. He then said he wanted to spend the rest of his days in God's service. Constantine attempted a return to Constantinople, making it only as far as a suburb of Nicomedia. He summoned the bishops, and told them of his hope to be baptized in the River Jordan, where Christ had been baptized. He requested the baptism right away.
The bishops fulfilled his wish. They sent him to River Jordan and there, the Arianizing bishop Eusebius of Nicomedia performed the sacred ceremonies according to custom. "I see the light of

God calling," Constantine said after the ceremony. He was filled with joy, and gave many thanks to God.

He then confirmed the division of the Empire among his sons. To the eldest, Constantine Junior, he assigned the government of the western parts of the Empire. His second son, Constantius, was constituted Emperor in the eastern division. And to his youngest son, Constans, he assigned the government of Illyria. He also granted many privileges to Rome and Constantinople. He placed his testament in the hands of the presbyter who constantly extolled Arius, and who had been recommended to him as a man of virtuous life by his sister Constantia in her last moments, and commanded him with an added oath to deliver it to Constantius on his return, for neither Constantius nor the other Emperors were with their dying father. After the making of this will, Constantine's health deteriorated.

***

As he lied in his death bed, Lactantius came to reassure him of God's promises to all who have believed in him and he told Constantine that God was waiting for him with open arms to receive him in his eternal kingdom.

"That cross of light you saw before the battle of the Milvian Bridge and again after your baptism will show you the way to the Father," Lactantius told Constantine.

"I know Jesus is the way, the truth, and the life. I die in peace because the truth set me free," said Constantine.

Meantime Constantine started praying the Lord's Prayer: "Our father who art in heaven. Blessed be thy name. Thy kingdom come. Thy will be done on earth, as it is in heaven." These were the last words Constantine said before he closed his eyes.

He died in the sixty-fifth year of his age, and the thirty-first of his reign at a suburban villa called Achyron, on the last day of the fifty-day festival of Pentecost directly following Easter, on May 22, 337.

With tears in his eyes, Lactantius wrote a letter to inform other bishops and believers about Constantine's death.

"The great Constantine was a powerful protector of the Christian religion, and was the first of the Emperors who was zealous for the Church, and bestowed upon it high benefactions. He was more successful than any other sovereign in all his undertakings; for he formed no design, I am convinced, without God. He was victorious in his wars against all enemies, even the Goths and Sarmatians, and, indeed, in all his military enterprises; and he changed the form of government according to his own mind with so much ease, that he created another senate and another imperial city, to which he gave his own name. Let us all join in the ceremonies which will take place in the Church of the Apostles, where we will have the chance to say farewell to this great man," Lactantius wrote.

Constantine's body was placed in a golden coffin before it was conveyed to Constantinople. As it arrived in the Imperial Palace, it was laid out on an elevated bed, surrounded by guards. In respect to his great deeds, the same honor and ceremonial were observed, by those who were in the palace, as were accorded to him, while living.

On hearing of his father's death, Constantius, who was then in the East, hastened to Constantinople. He paid great tribute to his late father and interred the royal remains with the utmost magnificence, and deposited them in the tomb which had been constructed by an order of the deceased, in the Church of the Apostles. The ceremony was attended by a great number of Bishops and simple Christian believers. As the golden coffin was being placed in the tomb, Lactantius made the sign of the cross. "He was a good Emperor," Lactantius said.

End